MY WIFE

Maupassant Original Short Stories

Volume VII

Guy de Maupassant

iBoo Press
London

MY WIFE

Maupassant Original Short Stories

Volume VII

Guy de Maupassant

Translated by
ALBERT M. C. McMASTER, B.A.
A. E. HENDERSON, B.A.
MME. QUESADA and Others

Published by
iBoo Press House

3rd Floor
86-90 Paul Street
London, EC2A4NE UK

t: +44 20 3695 0809
info@iboo.com II iBoo.com

ISBN
978-1-64181-745-5 (p)

We care about the environment. This paper used in this
publication is both acid free and totally chlorine-free (TCF).
It meets the minumum requirements of ANSI / NISO z39-
49-1992 (r 1997)

Printed in the United States

MY WIFE

Maupassant Original Short Stories

Volume VII

Guy de Maupassant

MY WIFE

Maupassant Original Short Stories

Volume-VII

Guy de Maupassant

VOLUME VII

THE FALSE GEMS

*M*onsieur Lantin had met the young girl at a reception at the house of the second head of his department, and had fallen head over heels in love with her.

She was the daughter of a provincial tax collector, who had been dead several years. She and her mother came to live in Paris, where the latter, who made the acquaintance of some of the families in her neighborhood, hoped to find a husband for her daughter.

They had very moderate means, and were honorable, gentle, and quiet.

The young girl was a perfect type of the virtuous woman in whose hands every sensible young man dreams of one day intrusting his happiness. Her simple beauty had the charm of angelic modesty, and the imperceptible smile which constantly hovered about the lips seemed to be the reflection of a pure and lovely soul. Her praises resounded on every side. People never tired of repeating: "Happy the man who wins her love! He could not find a better wife."

Monsieur Lantin, then chief clerk in the Department of the Interior, enjoyed a snug little salary of three thousand five hundred francs, and he proposed to this model young girl, and was accepted.

He was unspeakably happy with her. She governed his household with such clever economy that they seemed to live in luxury. She lavished the most delicate attentions on her husband, coaxed and fondled him; and so great was her charm that six years after their marriage, Monsieur Lantin discovered that he loved his wife even more than during the first days of their honeymoon.

He found fault with only two of her tastes: Her love for the theatre, and her taste for imitation jewelry. Her friends (the wives of some petty officials) frequently procured for her a box at the theatre, often for the first representations of the new plays; and her husband was obliged to accompany her, whether he wished it or not, to these entertainments which bored him excessively after his day's work at the office.

After a time, Monsieur Lantin begged his wife to request some lady of her acquaintance to accompany her, and to bring her home after the theatre. She opposed this arrangement, at first; but, after much persuasion, finally consented, to the infinite delight of her husband.

Now, with her love for the theatre, came also the desire for ornaments. Her costumes remained as before, simple, in good taste, and always modest; but she soon began to adorn her ears with huge rhinestones, which glittered and sparkled like real diamonds. Around her neck she wore strings of false pearls, on her arms bracelets of imitation gold, and combs set with glass jewels.

Her husband frequently remonstrated with her, saying:

"My dear, as you cannot afford to buy real jewelry, you ought to appear adorned with your beauty and modesty alone, which are the rarest ornaments of your sex."

But she would smile sweetly, and say:

"What can I do? I am so fond of jewelry. It is my only weakness. We cannot change our nature."

Then she would wind the pearl necklace round her fingers, make the facets of the crystal gems sparkle, and say:

"Look! are they not lovely? One would swear they were real."

Monsieur Lantin would then answer, smilingly:

"You have bohemian tastes, my dear."

Sometimes, of an evening, when they were enjoying a tete-a-tete by the fireside, she would place on the tea table the morocco leather box containing the "trash," as Monsieur Lantin called it. She would examine the false gems with a passionate attention, as though they imparted some deep and secret joy; and she often persisted in passing a necklace around her husband's neck, and, laughing heartily, would exclaim: "How droll you look!" Then she would throw herself into his arms, and kiss him affectionately.

One evening, in winter, she had been to the opera, and returned home chilled through and through. The next morning she coughed, and eight days later she died of inflammation of the lungs.

Monsieur Lantin's despair was so great that his hair became white in one month. He wept unceasingly; his heart was broken as he remembered her smile, her voice, every charm of his dead wife.

Time did not assuage his grief. Often, during office hours,

while his colleagues were discussing the topics of the day, his eyes would suddenly fill with tears, and he would give vent to his grief in heartrending sobs. Everything in his wife's room remained as it was during her lifetime; all her furniture, even her clothing, being left as it was on the day of her death. Here he was wont to seclude himself daily and think of her who had been his treasure-the joy of his existence.

But life soon became a struggle. His income, which, in the hands of his wife, covered all household expenses, was now no longer sufficient for his own immediate wants; and he wondered how she could have managed to buy such excellent wine and the rare delicacies which he could no longer procure with his modest resources.

He incurred some debts, and was soon reduced to absolute poverty. One morning, finding himself without a cent in his pocket, he resolved to sell something, and immediately the thought occurred to him of disposing of his wife's paste jewels, for he cherished in his heart a sort of rancor against these "deceptions," which had always irritated him in the past. The very sight of them spoiled, somewhat, the memory of his lost darling.

To the last days of her life she had continued to make purchases, bringing home new gems almost every evening, and he turned them over some time before finally deciding to sell the heavy necklace, which she seemed to prefer, and which, he thought, ought to be worth about six or seven francs; for it was of very fine workmanship, though only imitation.

He put it in his pocket, and started out in search of what seemed a reliable jeweler's shop. At length he found one, and went in, feeling a little ashamed to expose his misery, and also to offer such a worthless article for sale.

"Sir," said he to the merchant, "I would like to know what this is worth."

The man took the necklace, examined it, called his clerk, and made some remarks in an undertone; he then put the ornament back on the counter, and looked at it from a distance to judge of the effect.

Monsieur Lantin, annoyed at all these ceremonies, was on the point of saying: "Oh! I know well enough it is not worth anything," when the jeweler said: "Sir, that necklace is worth from twelve to fifteen thousand francs; but I could not buy it, unless you can tell me exactly where it came from."

The widower opened his eyes wide and remained gaping, not comprehending the merchant's meaning. Finally he stammered:

"You say—are you sure?" The other replied, drily: "You can try elsewhere and see if any one will offer you more. I consider it worth fifteen thousand at the most. Come back; here, if you cannot do better."

Monsieur Lantin, beside himself with astonishment, took up the necklace and left the store. He wished time for reflection.

Once outside, he felt inclined to laugh, and said to himself: "The fool! Oh, the fool! Had I only taken him at his word! That jeweler cannot distinguish real diamonds from the imitation article."

A few minutes after, he entered another store, in the Rue de la Paix. As soon as the proprietor glanced at the necklace, he cried out:

"Ah, parbleu! I know it well; it was bought here."

Monsieur Lantin, greatly disturbed, asked:

"How much is it worth?"

"Well, I sold it for twenty thousand francs. I am willing to take it back for eighteen thousand, when you inform me, according to our legal formality, how it came to be in your possession."

This time, Monsieur Lantin was dumfounded. He replied:

"But—but—examine it well. Until this moment I was under the impression that it was imitation."

The jeweler asked:

"What is your name, sir?"

"Lantin—I am in the employ of the Minister of the Interior. I live at number sixteen Rue des Martyrs."

The merchant looked through his books, found the entry, and said: "That necklace was sent to Madame Lantin's address, sixteen Rue des Martyrs, July 20, 1876."

The two men looked into each other's eyes—the widower speechless with astonishment; the jeweler scenting a thief. The latter broke the silence.

"Will you leave this necklace here for twenty-four hours?" said he; "I will give you a receipt."

Monsieur Lantin answered hastily: "Yes, certainly." Then, putting the ticket in his pocket, he left the store.

He wandered aimlessly through the streets, his mind in a state of dreadful confusion. He tried to reason, to understand. His wife could not afford to purchase such a costly ornament. Certainly not.

But, then, it must have been a present!—a present!—a present, from whom? Why was it given her?

He stopped, and remained standing in the middle of the street. A horrible doubt entered his mind—She? Then, all the other jewels must have been presents, too! The earth seemed to tremble beneath him—the tree before him to be falling; he threw up his arms, and fell to the ground, unconscious. He recovered his senses in a pharmacy, into which the passers-by had borne him. He asked to be taken home, and, when he reached the house, he shut himself up in his room, and wept until nightfall. Finally, overcome with fatigue, he went to bed and fell into a heavy sleep.

The sun awoke him next morning, and he began to dress slowly to go to the office. It was hard to work after such shocks. He sent a letter to his employer, requesting to be excused. Then he remembered that he had to return to the jeweler's. He did not like the idea; but he could not leave the necklace with that man. He dressed and went out.

It was a lovely day; a clear, blue sky smiled on the busy city below. Men of leisure were strolling about with their hands in their pockets.

Monsieur Lantin, observing them, said to himself: "The rich, indeed, are happy. With money it is possible to forget even the deepest sorrow. One can go where one pleases, and in travel find that distraction which is the surest cure for grief. Oh if I were only rich!"

He perceived that he was hungry, but his pocket was empty. He again remembered the necklace. Eighteen thousand francs! Eighteen thousand francs! What a sum!

He soon arrived in the Rue de la Paix, opposite the jeweler's. Eighteen thousand francs! Twenty times he resolved to go in, but shame kept him back. He was hungry, however—very hungry—and not a cent in his pocket. He decided quickly, ran across the street, in order not to have time for reflection, and rushed into the store.

The proprietor immediately came forward, and politely offered him a chair; the clerks glanced at him knowingly.

"I have made inquiries, Monsieur Lantin," said the jeweler, "and if you are still resolved to dispose of the gems, I am ready to pay you the price I offered."

"Certainly, sir," stammered Monsieur Lantin.

Whereupon the proprietor took from a drawer eighteen large bills, counted, and handed them to Monsieur Lantin, who signed a receipt; and, with trembling hand, put the money into his pocket.

As he was about to leave the store, he turned toward the merchant, who still wore the same knowing smile, and lowering his eyes, said:

"I have—I have other gems, which came from the same source. Will you buy them, also?"

The merchant bowed: "Certainly, sir."

Monsieur Lantin said gravely: "I will bring them to you." An hour later, he returned with the gems.

The large diamond earrings were worth twenty thousand francs; the bracelets, thirty-five thousand; the rings, sixteen thousand; a set of emeralds and sapphires, fourteen thousand; a gold chain with solitaire pendant, forty thousand—making the sum of one hundred and forty-three thousand francs.

The jeweler remarked, jokingly:

"There was a person who invested all her savings in precious stones."

Monsieur Lantin replied, seriously:

"It is only another way of investing one's money."

That day he lunched at Voisin's, and drank wine worth twenty francs a bottle. Then he hired a carriage and made a tour of the Bois. He gazed at the various turnouts with a kind of disdain, and could hardly refrain from crying out to the occupants:

"I, too, am rich!—I am worth two hundred thousand francs."

Suddenly he thought of his employer. He drove up to the bureau, and entered gaily, saying:

"Sir, I have come to resign my position. I have just inherited three hundred thousand francs."

He shook hands with his former colleagues, and confided to them some of his projects for the future; he then went off to dine at the Cafe Anglais.

He seated himself beside a gentleman of aristocratic bearing; and, during the meal, informed the latter confidentially that he had just inherited a fortune of four hundred thousand francs.

For the first time in his life, he was not bored at the theatre, and spent the remainder of the night in a gay frolic.

Six months afterward, he married again. His second wife was a very virtuous woman; but had a violent temper. She caused him much sorrow.

FASCINATION

*J*can tell you neither the name of the country, nor the name of the man. It was a long, long way from here on a fertile and burning shore. We had been walking since the morning along the coast, with the blue sea bathed in sunlight on one side of us, and the shore covered with crops on the other. Flowers were growing quite close to the waves, those light, gentle, lulling waves. It was very warm, a soft warmth permeated with the odor of the rich, damp, fertile soil. One fancied one was inhaling germs.

I had been told, that evening, that I should meet with hospitality at the house of a Frenchman who lived in an orange grove at the end of a promontory. Who was he? I did not know. He had come there one morning ten years before, and had bought land which he planted with vines and sowed with grain. He had worked, this man, with passionate energy, with fury. Then as he went on from month to month, year to year, enlarging his boundaries, cultivating incessantly the strong virgin soil, he accumulated a fortune by his indefatigable labor.

But he kept on working, they said. Rising at daybreak, he would remain in the fields till evening, superintending everything without ceasing, tormented by one fixed idea, the insatiable desire for money, which nothing can quiet, nothing satisfy. He now appeared to be very rich. The sun was setting as I reached his house. It was situated as described, at the end of a promontory in the midst of a grove of orange trees. It was a large square house, quite plain, and overlooked the sea. As I approached, a man wearing a long beard appeared in the doorway. Having greeted him, I asked if he would give me shelter for the night. He held out his hand and said, smiling:

"Come in, monsieur, consider yourself at home."

He led me into a room, and put a man servant at my disposal with the perfect ease and familiar graciousness of a man-of-the-world. Then he left me saying:

"We will dine as soon as you are ready to come downstairs."

We took dinner, sitting opposite each other, on a terrace facing the sea. I began to talk about this rich, distant, unknown land. He smiled, as he replied carelessly:

"Yes, this country is beautiful. But no country satisfies one when they are far from the one they love."

"You regret France?"

"I regret Paris."

"Why do you not go back?"

"Oh, I will return there."

And gradually we began to talk of French society, of the boulevards, and things Parisian. He asked me questions that showed he knew all about these things, mentioned names, all the familiar names in vaudeville known on the sidewalks.

"Whom does one see at Tortoni's now?

"Always the same crowd, except those who died." I looked at him attentively, haunted by a vague recollection. I certainly had seen that head somewhere. But where? And when? He seemed tired, although he was vigorous; and sad, although he was determined. His long, fair beard fell on his chest. He was somewhat bald and had heavy eyebrows and a thick mustache.

The sun was sinking into the sea, turning the vapor from the earth into a fiery mist. The orange blossoms exhaled their powerful, delicious fragrance. He seemed to see nothing besides me, and gazing steadfastly he appeared to discover in the depths of my mind the far-away, beloved and well-known image of the wide, shady pavement leading from the Madeleine to the Rue Drouot.

"Do you know Boutrelle?"

"Yes, indeed."

"Has he changed much?"

"Yes, his hair is quite white."

"And La Ridamie?"

"The same as ever."

"And the women? Tell me about the women. Let's see. Do you know Suzanne Verner?"

"Yes, very much. But that is over."

"Ah! And Sophie Astier?"

"Dead."

"Poor girl. Did you—did you know—"

But he ceased abruptly: And then, in a changed voice, his face suddenly turning pale, he continued:

"No, it is best that I should not speak of that any more, it breaks my heart."

Then, as if to change the current of his thoughts he rose.

"Would you like to go in?" he said.

"Yes, I think so."

And he preceded me into the house. The downstairs rooms were enormous, bare and mournful, and had a deserted look. Plates and glasses were scattered on the tables, left there by the dark-skinned servants who wandered incessantly about this spacious dwelling.

Two rifles were banging from two nails, on the wall; and in the corners of the rooms were spades, fishing poles, dried palm leaves, every imaginable thing set down at random when people came home in the evening and ready to hand when they went out at any time, or went to work.

My host smiled as he said:

"This is the dwelling, or rather the kennel, of an exile, but my own room is cleaner. Let us go there."

As I entered I thought I was in a second-hand store, it was so full of things of all descriptions, strange things of various kinds that one felt must be souvenirs. On the walls were two pretty paintings by well-known artists, draperies, weapons, swords and pistols, and exactly in the middle, on the principal panel, a square of white satin in a gold frame.

Somewhat surprised, I approached to look at it, and perceived a hairpin fastened in the centre of the glossy satin. My host placed his hand on my shoulder.

"That," said he, "is the only thing that I look at here, and the only thing that I have seen for ten years. M. Prudhomme said: 'This sword is the most memorable day of my life.' I can say: 'This hairpin is all my life.'"

I sought for some commonplace remark, and ended by saying:

"You have suffered on account of some woman?"

He replied abruptly:

"Say, rather, that I am suffering like a wretch."

"But come out on my balcony. A name rose to my lips just now which I dared not utter; for if you had said 'Dead' as you did of Sophie Astier, I should have fired a bullet into my brain, this very day."

We had gone out on the wide balcony from whence we could see two gulfs, one to the right and the other to the left, enclosed by high gray mountains. It was just twilight and the reflection of the sunset still lingered in the sky.

He continued:

"Is Jeanne de Limours still alive?"

His eyes were fastened on mine and were full of a trembling

anxiety. I smiled.

"Parbleu—she is prettier than ever."

"Do you know her?"

"Yes."

He hesitated and then said:

"Very well?"

"No."

He took my hand.

"Tell me about her," he said.

"Why, I have nothing to tell. She is one of the most charming women, or, rather, girls, and the most admired in Paris. She leads a delightful existence and lives like a princess, that is all."

"I love her," he murmured in a tone in which he might have said "I am going to die." Then suddenly he continued:

"Ah! For three years we lived in a state of terror and delight. I almost killed her five or six times. She tried to pierce my eyes with that hairpin that you saw just now. Look, do you see that little white spot beneath my left eye? We loved each other. How can I explain that infatuation? You would not understand it."

"There must be a simple form of love, the result of the mutual impulse of two hearts and two souls. But there is also assuredly an atrocious form, that tortures one cruelly, the result of the occult blending of two unlike personalities who detest each other at the same time that they adore one another."

"In three years this woman had ruined me. I had four million francs which she squandered in her calm manner, quietly, eat them up with a gentle smile that seemed to fall from her eyes on to her lips."

"You know her? There is something irresistible about her. What is it? I do not know. Is it those gray eyes whose glance penetrates you like a gimlet and remains there like the point of an arrow? It is more likely the gentle, indifferent and fascinating smile that she wears like a mask. Her slow grace pervades you little by little; exhales from her like a perfume, from her slim figure that scarcely sways as she passes you, for she seems to glide rather than walk; from her pretty voice with its slight drawl that would seem to be the music of her smile; from her gestures, also, which are never exaggerated, but always appropriate, and intoxicate your vision with their harmony. For three years she was the only being that existed for me on the earth! How I suffered; for she deceived me as she deceived everyone! Why? For no reason; just for the pleasure of deceiving. And when I found it out, when I treated her as a common girl and a beggar, she said quietly: 'Are we married?'

"Since I have been here I have thought so much about her that at last I understand her. She is Manon Lescaut come back to life. It is Marion, who could not love without deceiving; Marion for whom love, amusement, money, are all one."

He was silent. After a few minutes he resumed:

"When I had spent my last sou on her she said simply:

"'You understand, my dear boy, that I cannot live on air and weather. I love you very much, better than anyone, but I must live. Poverty and I could not keep house together.'

"And if I should tell you what a horrible life I led with her! When I looked at her I would just as soon have killed her as kissed her. When I looked at her . . . I felt a furious desire to open my arms to embrace and strangle her. She had, back of her eyes, something false and intangible that made me execrate her; and that was, perhaps, the reason I loved her so well. The eternal feminine, the odious and seductive feminine, was stronger in her than in any other woman. She was full of it, overcharged, as with a venomous and intoxicating fluid. She was a woman to a greater extent than any one has ever been."

"And when I went out with her she would look at all men in such a manner that she seemed to offer herself to each in a single glance. This exasperated me, and still it attached me to her all the more. This creature in just walking along the street belonged to everyone, in spite of me, in spite of herself, by the very fact of her nature, although she had a modest, gentle carriage. Do you understand?

"And what torture! At the theatre, at the restaurant she seemed to belong to others under my very eyes. And as soon as I left her she did belong to others.

"It is now ten years since I saw her and I love her better than ever."

Night spread over the earth. A strong perfume of orange blossoms pervaded the air. I said:

"Will you see her again?"

"Parbleu! I now have here, in land and money, seven to eight thousand francs. When I reach a million I shall sell out and go away. I shall have enough to live on with her for a year—one whole year. And then, good-bye, my life will be finished."

"But after that?" I asked.

"After that, I do not know. That will be all, I may possibly ask her to take me as a valet de chambre."

YVETTE SAMORIS

"The Comtesse Samoris."

"That lady in black over there?"

"The very one. She's wearing mourning for her daughter, whom she killed."

"You don't mean that seriously? How did she die?"

"Oh! it is a very simple story, without any crime in it, any violence."

"Then what really happened?"

"Almost nothing. Many courtesans are born to be virtuous women, they say; and many women called virtuous are born to be courtesans—is that not so? Now, Madame Samoris, who was born a courtesan, had a daughter born a virtuous woman, that's all."

"I don't quite understand you."

"I'll—explain what I mean. The comtesse is nothing but a common, ordinary parvenue originating no one knows where. A Hungarian or Wallachian countess or I know not what. She appeared one winter in apartments she had taken in the Champs Elysees, that quarter for adventurers and adventuresses, and opened her drawing-room to the first comer or to any one that turned up.

"I went there. Why? you will say. I really can't tell you. I went there, as every one goes to such places because the women are facile and the men are dishonest. You know that set composed of filibusters with varied decorations, all noble, all titled, all unknown at the embassies, with the exception of those who are spies. All talk of their honor without the slightest occasion for doing so, boast of their ancestors, tell you about their lives, braggarts, liars, sharpers, as dangerous as the false cards they have up their sleeves, as delusive as their names—in short, the aristocracy of the bagnio.

"I adore these people. They are interesting to study, interesting to know, amusing to understand, often clever, never commonplace like public functionaries. Their wives are always pretty, with a slight flavor of foreign roguery, with the mystery of their existence, half of it perhaps spent in a house of correction. They have, as a rule, magnificent eyes and incredible hair. I adore them also.

"Madame Samoris is the type of these adventuresses, elegant, mature and still beautiful. Charming feline creatures, you feel that they are vicious to the marrow of their bones. You find them very amusing when you visit them; they give card parties; they have dances and suppers; in short, they offer you all the pleasures of social life.

"And she had a daughter—a tall, fine-looking girl, always ready for amusement, always full of laughter and reckless gaiety—a true adventuress' daughter—but, at the same time, an innocent, unsophisticated, artless girl, who saw nothing, knew nothing, understood nothing of all the things that happened in her father's house.

"The girl was simply a puzzle to me. She was a mystery. She lived amid those infamous surroundings with a quiet, tranquil ease that was either terribly criminal or else the result of innocence. She sprang from the filth of that class like a beautiful flower fed on corruption."

"How do you know about them?"

"How do I know? That's the funniest part of the business! One morning there was a ring at my door, and my valet came up to tell me that M. Joseph Bonenthal wanted to speak to me. I said directly:

"'And who is this gentleman?' My valet replied: 'I don't know, monsieur; perhaps 'tis some one that wants employment.' And so it was. The man wanted me to take him as a servant. I asked him where he had been last. He answered: 'With the Comtesse Samoris.' 'Ah!' said I, 'but my house is not a bit like hers.' 'I know that well, monsieur,' he said, 'and that's the very reason I want to take service with monsieur. I've had enough of these people: a man may stay a little while with them, but he won't remain long with them.' I required an additional man servant at the time and so I took him.

"A month later Mademoiselle Yvette Samoris died mysteriously, and here are all the details of her death I could gather from Joseph, who got them from his sweetheart, the comtesse's chambermaid.

"It was a ball night, and two newly arrived guests were chatting behind a door. Mademoiselle Yvette, who had just been dancing, leaned against this door to get a little air.

"They did not see her approaching, but she heard what they were saying. And this was what they said:

"'But who is the father of the girl?'

"'A Russian, it appears; Count Rouvaloff. He never comes near the mother now.'

"'And who is the reigning prince to-day?'

"'That English prince standing near the window; Madame Samoris adores him. But her adoration of any one never lasts longer than a month or six weeks. Nevertheless, as you see, she has a large circle of admirers. All are called—and nearly all are chosen. That kind of thing costs a good deal, but—hang it, what can you expect?'

"'And where did she get this name of Samoris?'

"'From the only man perhaps that she ever loved—a Jewish banker from Berlin who goes by the name of Samuel Morris.'

"'Good. Thanks. Now that I know what kind of woman she is and have seen her, I'm off!'

"What a shock this was to the mind of a young girl endowed with all the instincts of a virtuous woman! What despair over-whelmed that simple soul! What mental tortures quenched her unbounded gaiety, her delightful laughter, her exultant satisfaction with life! What a conflict took place in that youthful heart up to the moment when the last guest had left! Those were things that Joseph could not tell me. But, the same night, Yvette abruptly entered her mother's room just as the comtesse was getting into bed, sent out the lady's maid, who was close to the door, and, standing erect and pale and with great staring eyes, she said:

"'Mamma, listen to what I heard a little while ago during the ball.'

"And she repeated word for word the conversation just as I told it to you.

"The comtesse was so stunned that she did not know what to say in reply at first. When she recovered her self-possession she denied everything and called God to witness that there was no truth in the story.

"The young girl went away, distracted but not convinced. And she began to watch her mother.

"I remember distinctly the strange alteration that then took place in her. She became grave and melancholy. She would fix on us her great earnest eyes as if she wanted to read what was at the bottom of our hearts. We did not know what to think of her and used to imagine that she was looking out for a husband.

"One evening she overheard her mother talking to her admirer and later saw them together, and her doubts were confirmed. She was heartbroken, and after telling her mother what she had seen, she said coldly, like a man of business laying down the terms of an agreement:

"'Here is what I have determined to do, mamma: We will both go away to some little town, or rather into the country. We will live there quietly as well as we can. Your jewelry alone may be called a fortune. If you wish to marry some honest man, so much the better; still better will it be if I can find one. If you don't consent to do this, I will kill myself.'

"This time the comtesse ordered her daughter to go to bed and never to speak again in this manner, so unbecoming in the mouth of a child toward her mother.

"Yvette's answer to this was: 'I give you a month to reflect. If, at the end of that month, we have not changed our way of living, I will kill myself, since there is no other honorable issue left to my life.'

"And she left the room.

"At the end of a month the Comtesse Samoris had resumed her usual entertainments, as though nothing had occurred. One day, under the pretext that she had a bad toothache, Yvette purchased a few drops of chloroform from a neighboring chemist. The next day she purchased more, and every time she went out she managed to procure small doses of the narcotic. She filled a bottle with it.

"One morning she was found in bed, lifeless and already quite cold, with a cotton mask soaked in chloroform over her face.

"Her coffin was covered with flowers, the church was hung in white. There was a large crowd at the funeral ceremony.

"Ah! well, if I had known—but you never can know—I would have married that girl, for she was infernally pretty."

"And what became of the mother?"

"Oh! she shed a lot of tears over it. She has only begun to receive visits again for the past week."

"And what explanation is given of the girl's death?"

"Oh! they pretended that it was an accident caused by a new stove, the mechanism of which got out of order. As a good many such accidents have occurred, the thing seemed probable enough."

A VENDETTA

The widow of Paolo Saverini lived alone with her son in a poor little house on the outskirts of Bonifacio. The town, built on an outjutting part of the mountain, in places even overhanging the sea, looks across the straits, full of sandbanks, towards the southernmost coast of Sardinia. Beneath it, on the other side and almost surrounding it, is a cleft in the cliff like an immense corridor which serves as a harbor, and along it the little Italian and Sardinian fishing boats come by a circuitous route between precipitous cliffs as far as the first houses, and every two weeks the old, wheezy steamer which makes the trip to Ajaccio.

On the white mountain the houses, massed together, makes an even whiter spot. They look like the nests of wild birds, clinging to this peak, overlooking this terrible passage, where vessels rarely venture. The wind, which blows uninterruptedly, has swept bare the forbidding coast; it drives through the narrow straits and lays waste both sides. The pale streaks of foam, clinging to the black rocks, whose countless peaks rise up out of the water, look like bits of rag floating and drifting on the surface of the sea.

The house of widow Saverini, clinging to the very edge of the precipice, looks out, through its three windows, over this wild and desolate picture.

She lived there alone, with her son Antonia and their dog "Semillante," a big, thin beast, with a long rough coat, of the sheepdog breed. The young man took her with him when out hunting.

One night, after some kind of a quarrel, Antoine Saverini was treacherously stabbed by Nicolas Ravolati, who escaped the same evening to Sardinia.

When the old mother received the body of her child, which the neighbors had brought back to her, she did not cry, but she stayed there for a long time motionless, watching him. Then, stretching her wrinkled hand over the body, she promised him a vendetta. She did not wish anybody near her, and she shut herself up beside the body with the dog, which howled continuously, standing at the foot of the bed, her head stretched towards her master and her tail between her legs. She did not move any more than did the mother, who, now leaning over the body with a blank stare, was weeping silently and watching it.

The young man, lying on his back, dressed in his jacket of coarse cloth, torn at the chest, seemed to be asleep. But he had blood all over him; on his shirt, which had been torn off in order to administer the first aid; on his vest, on his trousers, on his face, on his hands. Clots of blood had hardened in his beard and in his hair.

His old mother began to talk to him. At the sound of this voice the dog quieted down.

"Never fear, my boy, my little baby, you shall be avenged. Sleep, sleep; you shall be avenged. Do you hear? It's your mother's promise! And she always keeps her word, your mother does, you know she does."

Slowly she leaned over him, pressing her cold lips to his dead ones.

Then Semillante began to howl again with a long, monotonous, penetrating, horrible howl.

The two of them, the woman and the dog, remained there until morning.

Antoine Saverini was buried the next day and soon his name ceased to be mentioned in Bonifacio.

He had neither brothers nor cousins. No man was there to carry on the vendetta. His mother, the old woman, alone pondered over it.

On the other side of the straits she saw, from morning until night, a little white speck on the coast. It was the little Sardinian village Longosardo, where Corsican criminals take refuge when they are too closely pursued. They compose almost the entire population of this hamlet, opposite their native island, awaiting the time to return, to go back to the "maquis." She knew that Nicolas Ravolati had sought refuge in this village.

All alone, all day long, seated at her window, she was looking over there and thinking of revenge. How could she do anything without help—she, an invalid and so near death? But she had promised, she had sworn on the body. She could not forget, she could not wait. What could she do? She no longer slept at night; she had neither rest nor peace of mind; she thought persistently. The dog, dozing at her feet, would sometimes lift her head and howl. Since her master's death she often howled thus, as though she were calling him, as though her beast's soul, inconsolable too, had also retained a recollection that nothing could wipe out.

One night, as Semillante began to howl, the mother suddenly

got hold of an idea, a savage, vindictive, fierce idea. She thought it over until morning. Then, having arisen at daybreak she went to church. She prayed, prostrate on the floor, begging the Lord to help her, to support her, to give to her poor, broken-down body the strength which she needed in order to avenge her son.

She returned home. In her yard she had an old barrel, which acted as a cistern. She turned it over, emptied it, made it fast to the ground with sticks and stones. Then she chained Semillante to this improvised kennel and went into the house.

She walked ceaselessly now, her eyes always fixed on the distant coast of Sardinia. He was over there, the murderer.

All day and all night the dog howled. In the morning the old woman brought her some water in a bowl, but nothing more; no soup, no bread.

Another day went by. Semillante, exhausted, was sleeping. The following day her eyes were shining, her hair on end and she was pulling wildly at her chain.

All this day the old woman gave her nothing to eat. The beast, furious, was barking hoarsely. Another night went by.

Then, at daybreak, Mother Saverini asked a neighbor for some straw. She took the old rags which had formerly been worn by her husband and stuffed them so as to make them look like a human body.

Having planted a stick in the ground, in front of Semillante's kennel, she tied to it this dummy, which seemed to be standing up. Then she made a head out of some old rags.

The dog, surprised, was watching this straw man, and was quiet, although famished. Then the old woman went to the store and bought a piece of black sausage. When she got home she started a fire in the yard, near the kennel, and cooked the sausage. Semillante, frantic, was jumping about, frothing at the mouth, her eyes fixed on the food, the odor of which went right to her stomach.

Then the mother made of the smoking sausage a necktie for the dummy. She tied it very tight around the neck with string, and when she had finished she untied the dog.

With one leap the beast jumped at the dummy's throat, and with her paws on its shoulders she began to tear at it. She would fall back with a piece of food in her mouth, then would jump again, sinking her fangs into the string, and snatching few pieces of meat she would fall back again and once more spring forward. She was tearing up the face with her teeth and the whole neck was in tatters.

The old woman, motionless and silent, was watching eagerly.

Then she chained the beast up again, made her fast for two more days and began this strange performance again.

For three months she accustomed her to this battle, to this meal conquered by a fight. She no longer chained her up, but just pointed to the dummy.

She had taught her to tear him up and to devour him without even leaving any traces in her throat.

Then, as a reward, she would give her a piece of sausage.

As soon as she saw the man, Semillante would begin to tremble. Then she would look up to her mistress, who, lifting her finger, would cry, "Go!" in a shrill tone.

When she thought that the proper time had come, the widow went to confession and, one Sunday morning she partook of communion with an ecstatic fervor. Then, putting on men's clothes and looking like an old tramp, she struck a bargain with a Sardinian fisherman who carried her and her dog to the other side of the straits.

In a bag she had a large piece of sausage. Semillante had had nothing to eat for two days. The old woman kept letting her smell the food and whetting her appetite.

They got to Longosardo. The Corsican woman walked with a limp. She went to a baker's shop and asked for Nicolas Ravolati. He had taken up his old trade, that of carpenter. He was working alone at the back of his store.

The old woman opened the door and called:

"Hallo, Nicolas!"

He turned around. Then releasing her dog, she cried:

"Go, go! Eat him up! eat him up!"

The maddened animal sprang for his throat. The man stretched out his arms, clasped the dog and rolled to the ground. For a few seconds he squirmed, beating the ground with his feet. Then he stopped moving, while Semillante dug her fangs into his throat and tore it to ribbons. Two neighbors, seated before their door, remembered perfectly having seen an old beggar come out with a thin, black dog which was eating something that its master was giving him.

At nightfall the old woman was at home again. She slept well that night.

MY TWENTY-FIVE DAYS

*J*had just taken possession of my room in the hotel, a narrow den between two papered partitions, through which I could hear every sound made by my neighbors; and I was beginning to arrange my clothes and linen in the wardrobe with a long mirror, when I opened the drawer which is in this piece of furniture. I immediately noticed a roll of paper. Having opened it, I spread it out before me, and read this title:

My Twenty-five Days.

It was the diary of a guest at the watering place, of the last occupant of my room, and had been forgotten at the moment of departure.

These notes may be of some interest to sensible and healthy persons who never leave their own homes. It is for their benefit that I transcribe them without altering a letter.

"CHATEL-GUYON, July 15th.

"At the first glance it is not lively, this country. However, I am going to spend twenty-five days here, to have my liver and stomach treated, and to get thin. The twenty-five days of any one taking the baths are very like the twenty-eight days of the reserves; they are all devoted to fatigue duty, severe fatigue duty. To-day I have done nothing as yet; I have been getting settled. I have made the acquaintance of the locality and of the doctor. Chatel-Guyon consists of a stream in which flows yellow water, in the midst of several hillocks on which are a casino, some houses, and some stone crosses. On the bank of the stream, at the end of the valley, may be seen a square building surrounded by a little garden; this is the bathing establishment. Sad people wander around this building—the invalids. A great silence reigns in the walks shaded by trees, for this is not a pleasure resort, but a true health resort; one takes care of one's health as a business, and one gets well, so it seems.

"Those who know affirm, even, that the mineral springs perform true miracles here. However, no votive offering is hung around the cashier's office.

"From time to time a gentleman or a lady comes over to a kiosk with a slate roof, which shelters a woman of smiling and gentle aspect, and a spring boiling in a basin of cement: Not a word is exchanged between the invalid and the female custodian of the healing water. She hands the newcomer a little glass in which air bubbles sparkle in the transparent liquid. The guest drinks and goes off with a grave step to resume his interrupted walk beneath the trees.

"No noise in the little park, no breath of air in the leaves; no voice passes through this silence. One ought to write at the entrance to this district: 'No one laughs here; they take care of their health.'

"The people who chat resemble mutes who merely open their mouths to simulate sounds, so afraid are they that their voices might escape.

"In the hotel, the same silence. It is a big hotel, where you dine solemnly with people of good position, who have nothing to say to each other. Their manners bespeak good breeding, and their faces reflect the conviction of a superiority of which it might be difficult for some to give actual proofs.

"At two o'clock I made my way up to the Casino, a little wooden hut perched on a hillock, which one reaches by a goat path. But the view from that height is admirable. Chatel-Guyon is situated in a very narrow valley, exactly between the plain and the mountain. I perceive, at the left, the first great billows of the mountains of Auvergne, covered with woods, and here and there big gray patches, hard masses of lava, for we are at the foot of the extinct volcanoes. At the right, through the narrow cut of the valley, I discover a plain, infinite as the sea, steeped in a bluish fog which lets one only dimly discern the villages, the towns, the yellow fields of ripe grain, and the green squares of meadowland shaded with apple trees. It is the Limagne, an immense level, always enveloped in a light veil of vapor.

"The night has come. And now, after having dined alone, I write these lines beside my open window. I hear, over there, in front of me, the little orchestra of the Casino, which plays airs just as a foolish bird might sing all alone in the desert.

"A dog barks at intervals. This great calm does one good. Goodnight.

"July 16th.—Nothing new. I have taken a bath and then a shower bath. I have swallowed three glasses of water, and I have walked along the paths in the park, a quarter of an hour between each glass, then half an hour after the last. I have begun my twenty-five days.

"July 17th.—Remarked two mysterious, pretty women who are taking their baths and their meals after every one else has finished.

"July 18th.—Nothing new.

"July 19th.—Saw the two pretty women again. They have style and a little indescribable air which I like very much.

"July 20th.—Long walk in a charming wooded valley, as far as the Hermitage of Sans-Souci. This country is delightful, although sad; but so calm; so sweet, so green. One meets along the mountain roads long wagons loaded with hay, drawn by two cows at a slow pace or held back by them in going down the slopes with a great effort of their heads, which are yoked together. A man with a big black hat on his head is driving them with a slender stick, tipping them on the side or on the forehead; and often with a simple gesture, an energetic and serious gesture, he suddenly halts them when the excessive load precipitates their journey down the too rugged descents.

"The air is good to inhale in these valleys. And, if it is very warm, the dust bears with it a light odor of vanilla and of the stable, for so many cows pass over these routes that they leave reminders everywhere. And this odor is a perfume, when it would be a stench if it came from other animals.

"July 21st.—Excursion to the valley of the Enval. It is a narrow gorge inclosed by superb rocks at the very foot of the mountain. A stream flows amid the heaped-up boulders.

"As I reached the bottom of this ravine I heard women's voices, and I soon perceived the two mysterious ladies of my hotel, who were chatting, seated on a stone.

"The occasion appeared to me a good one, and I introduced myself without hesitation. My overtures were received without embarrassment. We walked back together to the hotel. And we talked about Paris. They knew, it seemed, many people whom I knew, too. Who can they be?

"I shall see them to-morrow. There is nothing more amusing than such meetings as this.

"July 22d.—Day passed almost entirely with the two unknown ladies. They are very pretty, by Jove!—one a brunette and the other a blonde. They say they are widows. H'm?

"I offered to accompany them to Royat tomorrow, and they accepted my offer.

"Chatel-Guyon is less sad than I thought on my arrival.

"July 23d.—Day spent at Royat. Royat is a little patch of hotels at the bottom of a valley, at the gate of Clermont-Ferrand. A great many people there. A large park full of life. Superb view of the Puyde-Dome, seen at the end of a perspective of valleys.

"My fair companions are very popular, which is flattering to me. The man who escorts a pretty woman always believes himself crowned with an aureole; with much more reason, the man who is accompanied by one on each side of him. Nothing is so pleasant as to dine in a fashionable restaurant with a female companion at whom everybody stares, and there is nothing better calculated to exalt a man in the estimation of his neighbors.

"To go to the Bois, in a trap drawn by a sorry nag, or to go out into the boulevard escorted by a plain woman, are the two most humiliating things that could happen to a sensitive heart that values the opinion of others. Of all luxuries, woman is the rarest and the most distinguished; she is the one that costs most and which we desire most; she is, therefore the one that we should seek by preference to exhibit to the jealous eyes of the world.

"To exhibit to the world a pretty woman leaning on your arm is to excite, all at once, every kind of jealousy. It is as much as to say: 'Look here! I am rich, since I possess this rare and costly object; I have taste, since I have known how to discover this pearl; perhaps, even, I am loved by her, unless I am deceived by her, which would still prove that others also consider her charming.

"But, what a disgrace it is to walk about town with an ugly woman!

"And how many humiliating things this gives people to understand!

"In the first place, they assume she must be your wife, for how could it be supposed that you would have an unattractive sweetheart? A true woman may be ungraceful; but then, her ugliness implies a thousand disagreeable things for you. One supposes you must be a notary or a magistrate, as these two professions have a monopoly of grotesque and well-dowered spouses. Now, is this not distressing to a man? And then, it seems to proclaim to the public that you have the odious courage, and are even under a legal obligation, to caress that ridiculous face and that ill-shaped body, and that you will, without doubt, be shameless enough to make a mother of this by no means desirable being—which is the very height of the ridiculous.

"July 24th.—I never leave the side of the two unknown widows, whom I am beginning to know quite well. This country is delightful and our hotel is excellent. Good season. The treatment is doing me an immense amount of good.

"July 25th.—Drive in a landau to the lake of Tazenat. An exquisite and unexpected jaunt decided on at luncheon. We started immediately on rising from table. After a long journey through the mountains we suddenly perceived an admirable little lake, quite round, very blue, clear as glass, and situated at the bottom of an extinct crater. One side of this immense basin is barren, the other is wooded. In the midst of the trees is a small house where sleeps a good-natured, intellectual man, a sage who passes his days in this Virgilian region. He opens his dwelling for us. An idea comes into my head. I exclaim:

"'Supposing we bathe?'

"'Yes,' they said, 'but costumes.'

"'Bah! we are in the wilderness.'

"And we did bathe!

"If I were a poet, how I would describe this unforgettable vision of those lissome young forms in the transparency of the water! The high, sloping sides shut in the lake, motionless, gleaming and round, as a silver coin; the sun pours into it a flood of warm light; and along the rocks the fair forms move in the almost invisible water in which the swimmers seemed suspended. On the sand at the bottom of the lake one could see their shadows as they moved along.

"July 26th.—Some persons seem to look with shocked and disapproving eyes at my rapid intimacy with the two fair widows. There are some people, then, who imagine that life consists in being bored. Everything that appears to be amusing becomes immediately a breach of good breeding or morality. For them duty has inflexible and mortally tedious rules.

"I would draw their attention, with all respect, to the fact that duty is not the same for Mormons, Arabs Zulus, Turks, Englishmen, and Frenchmen, and that there are very virtuous people among all these nations.

"I will cite a single example. As regards women, duty begins in England at nine years of age; in France at fifteen. As for me, I take a little of each people's notion of duty, and of the whole I make a result comparable to the morality of good King Solomon.

"July 27th.—Good news. I have lost 620 grams in weight. Excellent, this water of Chatel-Guyon! I am taking the widows to dine at Riom. A sad town whose anagram constitutes it an objectionable neighbor to healing springs: Riom, Mori.

"July 28th.—Hello, how's this! My two widows have been visited by two gentlemen who came to look for them. Two widowers, without doubt. They are leaving this evening. They have written to me on fancy notepaper.

"July 29th.—Alone! Long excursion on foot to the extinct crater of Nachere. Splendid view.

"July 30th.—Nothing. I am taking the treatment.

"July 31st.—Ditto. Ditto. This pretty country is full of polluted streams. I am drawing the notice of the municipality to the abominable sewer which poisons the road in front of the hotel. All the kitchen refuse of the establishment is thrown into it. This is a good way to breed cholera.

"August 1st.—Nothing. The treatment.

"August 2d.—Admirable walk to Chateauneuf, a place of sojourn for rheumatic patients, where everybody is lame. Nothing can be queerer than this population of cripples!

"August 3d.—Nothing. The treatment.

"August 4th.—Ditto. Ditto.

"August 5th.—Ditto. Ditto.

"August 6th.—Despair! I have just weighed myself. I have gained 310 grams. But then?

"August 7th.—Drove sixty-six kilometres in a carriage on the mountain. I will not mention the name of the country through respect for its women.

"This excursion had been pointed out to me as a beautiful one, and one that was rarely made. After four hours on the road, I arrived at a rather pretty village on the banks of a river in the midst of an admirable wood of walnut trees. I had not yet seen a forest of walnut trees of such dimensions in Auvergne. It constitutes, moreover, all the wealth of the district, for it is planted on the village common. This common was formerly only a hillside covered with brushwood. The authorities had tried in vain to get it cultivated. There was scarcely enough pasture on it to feed a few sheep.

"To-day it is a superb wood, thanks to the women, and it has a curious name: it is called the Sins of the Cure.

"Now I must say that the women of the mountain districts have the reputation of being light, lighter than in the plain. A bachelor who meets them owes them at least a kiss; and if he does not take more he is only a blockhead. If we consider this fairly, this way of looking at the matter is the only one that is logical and reasonable. As woman, whether she be of the town or the country, has her natural mission to please man, man should always show her that she pleases him. If he abstains from every sort of demonstration, this means that he considers her ugly; it is almost an insult to her. If I were a woman, I would not receive, a second time, a man who failed to show me respect at our first meeting, for I would consider that he had failed in appreciation of my beauty, my charm, and my feminine qualities.

"So the bachelors of the village X often proved to the women of the district that they found them to their taste, and, as the cure was unable to prevent these demonstrations, as gallant as they were natural, he resolved to utilize them for the benefit of the general prosperity. So he imposed as a penance on every woman who had gone wrong that she should plant a walnut tree on the common. And every night lanterns were seen moving about like will-o'-the-wisps on the hillock, for the erring ones scarcely like to perform their penance in broad daylight.

"In two years there was no longer any room on the lands belonging to the village, and to-day they calculate that there are more than three thousand trees around the belfry which rings out the services amid their foliage. These are the Sins of the Cure.

"Since we have been seeking for so many ways of rewooding France, the Administration of Forests might surely enter into some arrangement with the clergy to employ a method so simple as that employed by this humble cure.

"August 7th.—Treatment.

"August 8th.—I am packing up my trunks and saying good-by to the charming little district so calm and silent, to the green mountain, to the quiet valleys, to the deserted Casino, from which you can see, almost veiled by its light, bluish mist, the immense plain of the Limagne.

"I shall leave to-morrow."

Here the manuscript stopped. I will add nothing to it, my impressions of the country not having been exactly the same as those of my predecessor. For I did not find the two widows!

"THE TERROR"

*Y*ou say you cannot possibly understand it, and I believe you. You think I am losing my mind? Perhaps I am, but for other reasons than those you imagine, my dear friend.

Yes, I am going to be married, and will tell you what has led me to take that step.

I may add that I know very little of the girl who is going to become my wife to-morrow; I have only seen her four or five times. I know that there is nothing unpleasing about her, and that is enough for my purpose. She is small, fair, and stout; so, of course, the day after to-morrow I shall ardently wish for a tall, dark, thin woman.

She is not rich, and belongs to the middle classes. She is a girl such as you may find by the gross, well adapted for matrimony, without any apparent faults, and with no particularly striking qualities. People say of her:

"Mlle. Lajolle is a very nice girl," and tomorrow they will say: "What a very nice woman Madame Raymon is." She belongs, in a word, to that immense number of girls whom one is glad to have for one's wife, till the moment comes when one discovers that one happens to prefer all other women to that particular woman whom one has married.

"Well," you will say to me, "what on earth did you get married for?"

I hardly like to tell you the strange and seemingly improbable reason that urged me on to this senseless act; the fact, however, is that I am afraid of being alone.

I don't know how to tell you or to make you understand me, but my state of mind is so wretched that you will pity me and despise me.

I do not want to be alone any longer at night. I want to feel that there is some one close to me, touching me, a being who can speak and say something, no matter what it be.

I wish to be able to awaken somebody by my side, so that I may be able to ask some sudden question, a stupid question even, if

I feel inclined, so that I may hear a human voice, and feel that there is some waking soul close to me, some one whose reason is at work; so that when I hastily light the candle I may see some human face by my side—because—because —I am ashamed to confess it—because I am afraid of being alone.

Oh, you don't understand me yet.

I am not afraid of any danger; if a man were to come into the room, I should kill him without trembling. I am not afraid of ghosts, nor do I believe in the supernatural. I am not afraid of dead people, for I believe in the total annihilation of every being that disappears from the face of this earth.

Well—yes, well, it must be told: I am afraid of myself, afraid of that horrible sensation of incomprehensible fear.

You may laugh, if you like. It is terrible, and I cannot get over it. I am afraid of the walls, of the furniture, of the familiar objects; which are animated, as far as I am concerned, by a kind of animal life. Above all, I am afraid of my own dreadful thoughts, of my reason, which seems as if it were about to leave me, driven away by a mysterious and invisible agony.

At first I feel a vague uneasiness in my mind, which causes a cold shiver to run all over me. I look round, and of course nothing is to be seen, and I wish that there were something there, no matter what, as long as it were something tangible. I am frightened merely because I cannot understand my own terror.

If I speak, I am afraid of my own voice. If I walk, I am afraid of I know not what, behind the door, behind the curtains, in the cupboard, or under my bed, and yet all the time I know there is nothing anywhere, and I turn round suddenly because I am afraid of what is behind me, although there is nothing there, and I know it.

I become agitated. I feel that my fear increases, and so I shut myself up in my own room, get into bed, and hide under the clothes; and there, cowering down, rolled into a ball, I close my eyes in despair, and remain thus for an indefinite time, remembering that my candle is alight on the table by my bedside, and that I ought to put it out, and yet—I dare not do it.

It is very terrible, is it not, to be like that?

Formerly I felt nothing of all that. I came home quite calm, and went up and down my apartment without anything disturbing my peace of mind. Had any one told me that I should be attacked by a malady—for I can call it nothing else—of most improbable fear, such a stupid and terrible malady as it is, I should have laughed outright. I was certainly never afraid of opening the door in the dark. I went to bed slowly, without locking it, and never got up in the middle of the night to make sure that everything was firmly closed.

It began last year in a very strange manner on a damp autumn evening. When my servant had left the room, after I had dined, I asked myself what I was going to do. I walked up and down my room for some time, feeling tired without any reason for it, unable to work, and even without energy to read. A fine rain was falling, and I felt unhappy, a prey to one of those fits of despondency, without any apparent cause, which make us feel inclined to cry, or to talk, no matter to whom, so as to shake off our depressing thoughts.

I felt that I was alone, and my rooms seemed to me to be more empty than they had ever been before. I was in the midst of infinite and overwhelming solitude. What was I to do? I sat down, but a kind of nervous impatience seemed to affect my legs, so I got up and began to walk about again. I was, perhaps, rather feverish, for my hands, which I had clasped behind me, as one often does when walking slowly, almost seemed to burn one another. Then suddenly a cold shiver ran down my back, and I thought the damp air might have penetrated into my rooms, so I lit the fire for the first time that year, and sat down again and looked at the flames. But soon I felt that I could not possibly remain quiet, and so I got up again and determined to go out, to pull myself together, and to find a friend to bear me company.

I could not find anyone, so I walked to the boulevard to try and meet some acquaintance or other there.

It was wretched everywhere, and the wet pavement glistened in the gaslight, while the oppressive warmth of the almost impalpable rain lay heavily over the streets and seemed to obscure the light of the lamps.

I went on slowly, saying to myself: "I shall not find a soul to talk to."

I glanced into several cafes, from the Madeleine as far as the Faubourg Poissoniere, and saw many unhappy-looking individuals sitting at the tables who did not seem even to have enough energy left to finish the refreshments they had ordered.

For a long time I wandered aimlessly up and down, and about midnight I started for home. I was very calm and very tired. My janitor opened the door at once, which was quite unusual for him, and I thought that another lodger had probably just come in.

When I go out I always double-lock the door of my room, and I found it merely closed, which surprised me; but I supposed that some letters had been brought up for me in the course of the evening.

I went in, and found my fire still burning so that it lighted up the room a little, and, while in the act of taking up a candle, I noticed somebody sitting in my armchair by the fire, warming his feet, with his back toward me.

I was not in the slightest degree frightened. I thought, very naturally, that some friend or other had come to see me. No doubt the porter, to whom I had said I was going out, had lent him his own key. In a moment I remembered all the circumstances of my return, how the street door had been opened immediately, and that my own door was only latched and not locked.

I could see nothing of my friend but his head, and he had evidently gone to sleep while waiting for me, so I went up to him to rouse him. I saw him quite distinctly; his right arm was hanging down and his legs were crossed; the position of his head, which was somewhat inclined to the left of the armchair, seemed to indicate that he was asleep. "Who can it be?" I asked myself. I could not see clearly, as the room was rather dark, so I put out my hand to touch him on the shoulder, and it came in contact with the back of the chair. There was nobody there; the seat was empty.

I fairly jumped with fright. For a moment I drew back as if confronted by some terrible danger; then I turned round again, impelled by an imperious standing upright, panting with fear, so upset that I could not collect my thoughts, and ready to faint.

But I am a cool man, and soon recovered myself. I thought: "It is a mere hallucination, that is all," and I immediately began to reflect on this phenomenon. Thoughts fly quickly at such moments.

I had been suffering from an hallucination, that was an incontestable fact. My mind had been perfectly lucid and had acted regularly and logically, so there was nothing the matter with the brain. It was only my eyes that had been deceived; they had had a vision, one of those visions which lead simple folk to believe in miracles. It was a nervous seizure of the optical apparatus, nothing more; the eyes were rather congested, perhaps.

I lit my candle, and when I stooped down to the fire in doing so I noticed that I was trembling, and I raised myself up with a jump, as if somebody had touched me from behind.

I was certainly not by any means calm.

I walked up and down a little, and hummed a tune or two. Then I double-locked the door and felt rather reassured; now, at any rate, nobody could come in.

I sat down again and thought over my adventure for a long time; then I went to bed and blew out my light.

For some minutes all went well; I lay quietly on my back, but presently an irresistible desire seized me to look round the room, and I turned over on my side.

My fire was nearly out, and the few glowing embers threw a faint light on the floor by the chair, where I fancied I saw the man sitting again.

I quickly struck a match, but I had been mistaken; there was nothing there. I got up, however, and hid the chair behind my bed, and tried to get to sleep, as the room was now dark; but I had not forgotten myself for more than five minutes, when in my dream I saw all the scene which I had previously witnessed as clearly as if it were reality. I woke up with a start, and having lit the candle, sat up in bed, without venturing even to try to go to sleep again.

Twice, however, sleep overcame me for a few moments in spite of myself, and twice I saw the same thing again, till I fancied I was going mad. When day broke, however, I thought that I was cured, and slept peacefully till noon.

It was all past and over. I had been feverish, had had the nightmare. I know not what. I had been ill, in fact, but yet thought I was a great fool.

I enjoyed myself thoroughly that evening. I dined at a restaurant and afterward went to the theatre, and then started for home. But as I got near the house I was once more seized by a strange feeling of uneasiness. I was afraid of seeing him again. I was not afraid of him, not afraid of his presence, in which I did not believe; but I was afraid of being deceived again. I was afraid of some fresh hallucination, afraid lest fear should take possession of me.

For more than an hour I wandered up and down the pavement; then, feeling that I was really too foolish, I returned home. I breathed so hard that I could hardly get upstairs, and remained standing outside my door for more than ten minutes; then suddenly I had a courageous impulse and my will asserted itself. I inserted my key into the lock, and went into the apartment with a candle in my hand. I kicked open my bedroom door, which was partly open, and cast a frightened glance toward the fireplace. There was nothing there. A-h! What a relief and what a delight! What a deliverance! I walked up and down briskly and boldly, but I was not altogether reassured, and kept turning round with a jump; the very shadows in the corners disquieted me.

I slept badly, and was constantly disturbed by imaginary noises, but did not see him; no, that was all over.

Since that time I have been afraid of being alone at night. I feel that the spectre is there, close to me, around me; but it has not appeared to me again.

And supposing it did, what would it matter, since I do not believe in it, and know that it is nothing?

However, it still worries me, because I am constantly thinking of it. His right arm hanging down and his head inclined to the left like a man who was asleep—I don't want to think about it!

Why, however, am I so persistently possessed with this idea? His feet were close to the fire!

He haunts me; it is very stupid, but who and what is he? I know that he does not exist except in my cowardly imagination, in my fears, and in my agony. There—enough of that!

Yes, it is all very well for me to reason with myself, to stiffen my backbone, so to say; but I cannot remain at home because I know he is there. I know I shall not see him again; he will not show himself again; that is all over. But he is there, all the same, in my thoughts. He remains invisible, but that does not prevent his being there. He is behind the doors, in the closed cupboard, in the wardrobe, under the bed, in every dark corner. If I open the door or the cupboard, if I take the candle to look under the bed and throw a light on the dark places he is there no longer, but I feel that he is behind me. I turn round, certain that I shall not see him, that I shall never see him again; but for all that, he is behind me.

It is very stupid, it is dreadful; but what am I to do? I cannot help it.

But if there were two of us in the place I feel certain that he would not be there any longer, for he is there just because I am alone, simply and solely because I am alone!

LEGEND OF MONT ST. MICHEL

J had first seen it from Cancale, this fairy castle in the sea. I got an indistinct impression of it as of a gray shadow outlined against the misty sky. I saw it again from Avranches at sunset. The immense stretch of sand was red, the horizon was red, the whole boundless bay was red. The rocky castle rising out there in the distance like a weird, seignorial residence, like a dream palace, strange and beautiful-this alone remained black in the crimson light of the dying day.

The following morning at dawn I went toward it across the sands, my eyes fastened on this, gigantic jewel, as big as a mountain, cut like a cameo, and as dainty as lace. The nearer I approached the greater my admiration grew, for nothing in the world could be more wonderful or more perfect.

As surprised as if I had discovered the habitation of a god, I wandered through those halls supported by frail or massive columns, raising my eyes in wonder to those spires which looked like rockets starting for the sky, and to that marvellous assemblage of towers, of gargoyles, of slender and charming ornaments, a regular fireworks of stone, granite lace, a masterpiece of colossal and delicate architecture.

As I was looking up in ecstasy a Lower Normandy peasant came up to me and told me the story of the great quarrel between Saint Michael and the devil.

A sceptical genius has said: "God made man in his image and man has returned the compliment."

This saying is an eternal truth, and it would be very curious to write the history of the local divinity of every continent as well as the history of the patron saints in each one of our provinces. The negro has his ferocious man-eating idols; the polygamous Mahometan fills his paradise with women; the Greeks, like a practical people, deified all the passions.

Every village in France is under the influence of some protecting saint, modelled according to the characteristics of the inhabitants.

Saint Michael watches over Lower Normandy, Saint Michael,

the radiant and victorious angel, the sword-carrier, the hero of Heaven, the victorious, the conqueror of Satan.

But this is how the Lower Normandy peasant, cunning, deceitful and tricky, understands and tells of the struggle between the great saint and the devil.

To escape from the malice of his neighbor, the devil, Saint Michael built himself, in the open ocean, this habitation worthy of an archangel; and only such a saint could build a residence of such magnificence.

But as he still feared the approaches of the wicked one, he surrounded his domains by quicksands, more treacherous even than the sea.

The devil lived in a humble cottage on the hill, but he owned all the salt marshes, the rich lands where grow the finest crops, the wooded valleys and all the fertile hills of the country, while the saint ruled only over the sands. Therefore Satan was rich, whereas Saint Michael was as poor as a church mouse.

After a few years of fasting the saint grew tired of this state of affairs and began to think of some compromise with the devil, but the matter was by no means easy, as Satan kept a good hold on his crops.

He thought the thing over for about six months; then one morning he walked across to the shore. The demon was eating his soup in front of his door when he saw the saint. He immediately rushed toward him, kissed the hem of his sleeve, invited him in and offered him refreshments.

Saint Michael drank a bowl of milk and then began: "I have come here to propose to you a good bargain."

The devil, candid and trustful, answered: "That will suit me."

"Here it is. Give me all your lands."

Satan, growing alarmed, wished to speak "But—"

The saint continued: "Listen first. Give me all your lands. I will take care of all the work, the ploughing, the sowing, the fertilizing, everything, and we will share the crops equally. How does that suit you?"

The devil, who was naturally lazy, accepted. He only demanded in addition a few of those delicious gray mullet which are caught around the solitary mount. Saint Michael promised the fish.

They grasped hands and spat on the ground to show that it was a bargain, and the saint continued: "See here, so that you will have nothing to complain of, choose that part of the crops which you prefer: the part that grows above ground or the part that stays in the ground." Satan cried out: "I will take all that will be above ground."

"It's a bargain!" said the saint. And he went away.

Six months later, all over the immense domain of the devil, one could see nothing but carrots, turnips, onions, salsify, all the plants whose juicy roots are good and savory and whose useless leaves are good for nothing but for feeding animals.

Satan wished to break the contract, calling Saint Michael a swindler.

But the saint, who had developed quite a taste for agriculture, went back to see the devil and said:

"Really, I hadn't thought of that at all; it was just an accident, no fault of mine. And to make things fair with you, this year I'll let you take everything that is under the ground."

"Very well," answered Satan.

The following spring all the evil spirit's lands were covered with golden wheat, oats as big as beans, flax, magnificent colza, red clover, peas, cabbage, artichokes, everything that develops into grains or fruit in the sunlight.

Once more Satan received nothing, and this time he completely lost his temper. He took back his fields and remained deaf to all the fresh propositions of his neighbor.

A whole year rolled by. From the top of his lonely manor Saint Michael looked at the distant and fertile lands and watched the devil direct the work, take in his crops and thresh the wheat. And he grew angry, exasperated at his powerlessness.

As he was no longer able to deceive Satan, he decided to wreak vengeance on him, and he went out to invite him to dinner for the following Monday.

"You have been very unfortunate in your dealings with me," he said; "I know it, but I don't want any ill feeling between us, and I expect you to dine with me. I'll give you some good things to eat."

Satan, who was as greedy as he was lazy, accepted eagerly. On the day appointed he donned his finest clothes and set out for the castle.

Saint Michael sat him down to a magnificent meal. First there was a 'vol-au-vent', full of cocks' crests and kidneys, with meatballs, then two big gray mullet with cream sauce, a turkey stuffed with chestnuts soaked in wine, some salt-marsh lamb as tender as cake, vegetables which melted in the mouth and nice hot pancake which was brought on smoking and spreading a delicious odor of butter.

They drank new, sweet, sparkling cider and heady red wine,

and after each course they whetted their appetites with some old apple brandy.

The devil drank and ate to his heart's content; in fact he took so much that he was very uncomfortable, and began to retch.

Then Saint Michael arose in anger and cried in a voice like thunder: "What! before me, rascal! You dare—before me—"

Satan, terrified, ran away, and the saint, seizing a stick, pursued him. They ran through the halls, turning round the pillars, running up the staircases, galloping along the cornices, jumping from gargoyle to gargoyle. The poor devil, who was woefully ill, was running about madly and trying hard to escape. At last he found himself at the top of the last terrace, right at the top, from which could be seen the immense bay, with its distant towns, sands and pastures. He could no longer escape, and the saint came up behind him and gave him a furious kick, which shot him through space like a cannonball.

He shot through the air like a javelin and fell heavily before the town of Mortain. His horns and claws stuck deep into the rock, which keeps through eternity the traces of this fall of Satan.

He stood up again, limping, crippled until the end of time, and as he looked at this fatal castle in the distance, standing out against the setting sun, he understood well that he would always be vanquished in this unequal struggle, and he went away limping, heading for distant countries, leaving to his enemy his fields, his hills, his valleys and his marshes.

And this is how Saint Michael, the patron saint of Normandy, vanquished the devil.

Another people would have dreamed of this battle in an entirely different manner.

A NEW YEAR'S GIFT

*J*acques de Randal, having dined at home alone, told his valet he might go out, and he sat down at his table to write some letters.

He ended every year in this manner, writing and dreaming. He reviewed the events of his life since last New Year's Day, things that were now all over and dead; and, in proportion as the faces of his friends rose up before his eyes, he wrote them a few lines, a cordial New Year's greeting on the first of January.

So he sat down, opened a drawer, took out of it a woman's photograph, gazed at it a few moments, and kissed it. Then, having laid it beside a sheet of notepaper, he began:

"MY DEAR IRENE: You must by this time have received the little souvenir I sent you addressed to the maid. I have shut myself up this evening in order to tell you — — "

The pen here ceased to move. Jacques rose up and began walking up and down the room.

For the last ten months he had had a sweetheart, not like the others, a woman with whom one engages in a passing intrigue, of the theatrical world or the demi-monde, but a woman whom he loved and won. He was no longer a young man, although he was still comparatively young for a man, and he looked on life seriously in a positive and practical spirit.

Accordingly, he drew up the balance sheet of his passion, as he drew up every year the balance sheet of friendships that were ended or freshly contracted, of circumstances and persons that had entered into his life.

His first ardor of love having grown calmer, he asked himself with the precision of a merchant making a calculation what was the state of his heart with regard to her, and he tried to form an idea of what it would be in the future.

He found there a great and deep affection, made up of tenderness, gratitude and the thousand subtleties which give birth to long and powerful attachments.

A ring at the bell made him start. He hesitated. Should he open the door? But he said to himself that one must always open the door on New Year's night, to admit the unknown who is passing by and knocks, no matter who it may be.

So he took a wax candle, passed through the antechamber, drew back the bolts, turned the key, pulled the door back, and saw his sweetheart standing pale as a corpse, leaning against the wall.

He stammered:

"What is the matter with you?"

She replied:

"Are you alone?"

"Yes."

"Without servants?"

"Yes."

"You are not going out?"

"No."

She entered with the air of a woman who knew the house. As soon as she was in the drawing-room, she sank down on the sofa, and, covering her face with her hands, began to weep bitterly.

He knelt down at her feet, and tried to remove her hands from her eyes, so that he might look at them, and exclaimed:

"Irene, Irene, what is the matter with you? I implore you to tell me what is the matter with you?"

Then, amid her sobs, she murmured:

"I can no longer live like this."

"Live like this? What do you mean?"

"Yes. I can no longer live like this. I have endured so much. He struck me this afternoon."

"Who? Your husband?"

"Yes, my husband."

"Ah!"

He was astonished, having never suspected that her husband could be brutal. He was a man of the world, of the better class, a clubman, a lover of horses, a theatergoer and an expert swordsman; he was known, talked about, appreciated everywhere, having very courteous manners, a very mediocre intellect, an absence of education and of the real culture needed in order to think like all well-bred people, and finally a respect for conventionalities.

He appeared to devote himself to his wife, as a man ought to do in the case of wealthy and well-bred people. He displayed enough of anxiety about her wishes, her health, her dresses, and, beyond that, left her perfectly free.

Randal, having become Irene's friend, had a right to the affectionate hand-clasp which every husband endowed with good manners owes to his wife's intimate acquaintance. Then, when Jacques, after having been for some time the friend, became the lover, his relations with the husband were more cordial, as is fitting.

Jacques had never dreamed that there were storms in this household, and he was bewildered at this unexpected revelation.

He asked:

"How did it happen? Tell me."

Thereupon she related a long story, the entire history of her life since the day of her marriage, the first disagreement arising out of a mere nothing, then becoming accentuated at every new difference of opinion between two dissimilar dispositions.

Then came quarrels, a complete separation, not apparent, but real; next, her husband showed himself aggressive, suspicious, violent. Now, he was jealous, jealous of Jacques, and that very day, after a scene, he had struck her.

She added with decision: "I will not go back to him. Do with me what you like."

Jacques sat down opposite to her, their knees touching. He took her hands:

"My dear love, you are going to commit a gross, an irreparable folly. If you want to leave your husband, put him in the wrong, so that your position as a woman of the world may be saved."

She asked, as she looked at him uneasily:

"Then, what do you advise me?"

"To go back home and to put up with your life there till the day when you can obtain either a separation or a divorce, with the honors of war."

"Is not this thing which you advise me to do a little cowardly?"

"No; it is wise and sensible. You have a high position, a reputation to protect, friends to preserve and relations to deal with. You must not lose all these through a mere caprice."

She rose up, and said with violence:

"Well, no! I cannot stand it any longer! It is at an end! it is at an end!"

Then, placing her two hands on her lover's shoulders, and looking him straight in the face, she asked:

"Do you love me?"

"Yes."

"Really and truly?"

"Yes."

"Then take care of me."

He exclaimed:

"Take care of you? In my own house? Here? Why, you are mad. It would mean losing you forever; losing you beyond hope of recall! You are mad!"

She replied, slowly and seriously, like a woman who feels the weight of her words:

"Listen, Jacques. He has forbidden me to see you again, and I will not play this comedy of coming secretly to your house. You must either lose me or take me."

"My dear Irene, in that case, obtain your divorce, and I will marry you."

"Yes, you will marry me in—two years at the soonest. Yours is a patient love."

"Look here! Reflect! If you remain here he'll come to-morrow to take you away, seeing that he is your husband, seeing that he has right and law on his side."

"I did not ask you to keep me in your own house, Jacques, but to take me anywhere you like. I thought you loved me enough to do that. I have made a mistake. Good-by!"

She turned round and went toward the door so quickly that he was only able to catch hold of her when she was outside the room:

"Listen, Irene."

She struggled, and would not listen to him. Her eyes were full of tears, and she stammered:

"Let me alone! let me alone! let me alone!"

He made her sit down by force, and once more falling on his knees at her feet, he now brought forward a number of arguments and counsels to make her understand the folly and terrible risk of her project. He omitted nothing which he deemed necessary to convince her, finding even in his very affection for her incentives to persuasion.

As she remained silent and cold as ice, he begged of her, implored of her to listen to him, to trust him, to follow his advice.

When he had finished speaking, she only replied:

"Are you disposed to let me go away now? Take away your hands, so that I may rise to my feet."

"Look here, Irene."

"Will you let me go?"

"Irene—is your resolution irrevocable?"

"Will you let me go."

"Tell me only whether this resolution, this mad resolution of yours, which you will bitterly regret, is irrevocable?"

"Yes—let me go!"

"Then stay. You know well that you are at home here. We shall go away to-morrow morning."

She rose to her feet in spite of him, and said in a hard tone:

"No. It is too late. I do not want sacrifice; I do not want devotion."

"Stay! I have done what I ought to do; I have said what I ought to say. I have no further responsibility on your behalf. My conscience is at peace. Tell me what you want me to do, and I will obey."'

She resumed her seat, looked at him for a long time, and then asked, in a very calm voice:

"Well, then, explain."

"Explain what? What do you wish me to explain?"

"Everything—everything that you thought about before changing your mind. Then I will see what I ought to do."

"But I thought about nothing at all. I had to warn you that you were going to commit an act of folly. You persist; then I ask to share in this act of folly, and I even insist on it."

"It is not natural to change one's mind so quickly."

"Listen, my dear love. It is not a question here of sacrifice or devotion. On the day when I realized that I loved you, I said to myself what every lover ought to say to himself in the same case: 'The man who loves a woman, who makes an effort to win her, who gets her, and who takes her, enters into a sacred contract with himself and with her. That is, of course, in dealing with a woman like you, not a woman with a fickle heart and easily impressed.'

"Marriage which has a great social value, a great legal value, possesses in my eyes only a very slight moral value, taking into account the conditions under which it generally takes place.

"Therefore, when a woman, united by this lawful bond, but having no attachment to her husband, whom she cannot love, a woman whose heart is free, meets a man whom she cares for, and gives herself to him, when a man who has no other tie, takes a woman in this way, I say that they pledge themselves toward each other by this mutual and free agreement much more than by the 'Yes' uttered in the presence of the mayor.

"I say that, if they are both honorable persons, their union must be more intimate, more real, more wholesome, than if all the sacraments had consecrated it.

"This woman risks everything. And it is exactly because she knows it, because she gives everything, her heart, her body, her soul, her honor, her life, because she has foreseen all miseries, all dangers all catastrophes, because she dares to do a bold act, an intrepid act, because she is prepared, determined to brave everything—her husband, who might kill her, and society, which may cast her out. This is why she is worthy of respect in the midst of her conjugal infidelity; this is why her lover, in taking her, should also foresee everything, and prefer her to every one else whatever may happen. I have nothing more to say. I spoke in the beginning like a sensible man whose duty it was to warn you; and now I am only a man—a man who loves you—Command, and I obey."

Radiant, she closed his mouth with a kiss, and said in a low tone: "It is not true, darling! There is nothing the matter! My husband does not suspect anything. But I wanted to see, I wanted to know, what you would do. I wished for a New Year's gift—the gift of your heart—another gift besides the necklace you sent me. You have given it to me. Thanks! thanks! God be thanked for the happiness you have given me!"

FRIEND PATIENCE

What became of Leremy?"

"He is captain in the Sixth Dragoons."

"And Pinson?"

"He's a subprefect."

"And Racollet?"

"Dead."

We were searching for other names which would remind us of the youthful faces of our younger days. Once in a while we had met some of these old comrades, bearded, bald, married, fathers of several children, and the realization of these changes had given us an unpleasant shudder, reminding us how short life is, how everything passes away, how everything changes. My friend asked me:

"And Patience, fat Patience?"

I almost, howled:

"Oh! as for him, just listen to this. Four or five years ago I was in Limoges, on a tour of inspection, and I was waiting for dinner time. I was seated before the big cafe in the Place du Theatre, just bored to death. The tradespeople were coming by twos, threes or fours, to take their absinthe or vermouth, talking all the time of their own or other people's business, laughing loudly, or lowering their voices in order to impart some important or delicate piece of news.

"I was saying to myself: 'What shall I do after dinner?' And I thought of the long evening in this provincial town, of the slow, dreary walk through unknown streets, of the impression of deadly gloom which these provincial people produce on the lonely traveller, and of the whole oppressive atmosphere of the place.

"I was thinking of all these things as I watched the little jets of gas flare up, feeling my loneliness increase with the falling shadows.

"A big, fat man sat down at the next table and called in a stentorian voice:

"'Waiter, my bitters!'

"The 'my' came out like the report of a cannon. I immediately understood that everything was his in life, and not another's; that he had his nature, by Jove, his appetite, his trousers, his everything, his, more absolutely and more completely than anyone else's. Then he looked round him with a satisfied air. His bitters were brought, and he ordered:

"'My newspaper!'

"I wondered: 'Which newspaper can his be?' The title would certainly reveal to me his opinions, his theories, his principles, his hobbies, his weaknesses.

"The waiter brought the Temps. I was surprised. Why the Temps, a serious, sombre, doctrinaire, impartial sheet? I thought:

"'He must be a serious man with settled and regular habits; in short, a good bourgeois.'

"He put on his gold-rimmed spectacles, leaned back before beginning to read, and once more glanced about him. He noticed me, and immediately began to stare at me in an annoying manner. I was even going to ask the reason for this attention, when he exclaimed from his seat:

"'Well, by all that's holy, if this isn't Gontran Lardois.'

"I answered:

"'Yes, monsieur, you are not mistaken.'

"Then he quickly rose and came toward me with hands outstretched:

"'Well, old man, how are you?'

"As I did not recognize him at all I was greatly embarrassed. I stammered:

"'Why-very well-and-you?'

"He began to laugh "'I bet you don't recognize me.'

"'No, not exactly. It seems—however—'

"He slapped me on the back:

"'Come on, no joking! I am Patience, Robert Patience, your friend, your chum.'

"I recognized him. Yes, Robert Patience, my old college chum. It was he. I took his outstretched hand:

"'And how are you?'

"'Fine!'

"His smile was like a paean of victory.

"He asked:

"'What are you doing here?'

"I explained that I was government inspector of taxes.

"He continued, pointing to my red ribbon:

"'Then you have-been a success?'

"I answered:

"'Fairly so. And you?'

"'I am doing well!'

"'What are you doing?'

"'I'm in business.'

"'Making money?'

"'Heaps. I'm very rich. But come around to lunch, to-morrow noon, 17 Rue du Coq-qui-Chante; you will see my place.'

"He seemed to hesitate a second, then continued:

"'Are you still the good sport that you used to be?'

"'I—I hope so.'

"'Not married?'

"'No.'

"'Good. And do you still love a good time and potatoes?'

"I was beginning to find him hopelessly vulgar. Nevertheless, I answered "'Yes.'

"'And pretty girls?'

"'Most assuredly.'

"He began to laugh good-humoredly.

"'Good, good! Do you remember our first escapade, in Bordeaux, after that dinner at Routie's? What a spree!'

"I did, indeed, remember that spree; and the recollection of it cheered me up. This called to mind other pranks. He would say:

"'Say, do you remember the time when we locked the proctor up in old man Latoque's cellar?'

"And he laughed and banged the table with his fist, and then he continued:

"'Yes-yes-yes-and do you remember the face of the geography teacher, M. Marin, the day we set off a firecracker in the globe, just as he was haranguing about the principal volcanoes of the earth?'

"Then suddenly I asked him:

"'And you, are you married?'

"He exclaimed:

"'Ten years, my boy, and I have four children, remarkable youngsters; but you'll see them and their mother.'

"We were talking rather loud; the people around us looked at us in surprise.

"Suddenly my friend looked at his watch, a chronometer the size of a pumpkin, and he cried:

"'Thunder! I'm sorry, but I'll have to leave you; I am never free at night.'

"He rose, took both my hands, shook them as though he were trying to wrench my arms from their sockets, and exclaimed:

"'So long, then; till to-morrow noon!'

"'So long!'

"I spent the morning working in the office of the collector-general of the Department. The chief wished me to stay to luncheon, but I told him that I had an engagement with a friend. As he had to go out, he accompanied me.

"I asked him:

"'Can you tell me how I can find the Rue du Coq-qui-Chante?'

"He answered:

"'Yes, it's only five minutes' walk from here. As I have nothing special to do, I will take you there.'

"We started out and soon found ourselves there. It was a wide, fine-looking street, on the outskirts of the town. I looked at the houses and I noticed No. 17. It was a large house with a garden behind it. The facade, decorated with frescoes, in the Italian style, appeared to me as being in bad taste. There were goddesses holding vases, others swathed in clouds. Two stone cupids supported the number of the house.

"I said to the treasurer:

"'Here is where I am going.'

"I held my hand out to him. He made a quick, strange gesture, said nothing and shook my hand.

"I rang. A maid appeared. I asked:

"'Monsieur Patience, if you please?'

"She answered:

"'Right here, sir. Is it to monsieur that you wish to speak?'

"'Yes.'

"The hall was decorated with paintings from the brush of some local artist. Pauls and Virginias were kissing each other under palm trees bathed in a pink light. A hideous Oriental lantern was ranging from the ceiling. Several doors were concealed by bright hangings.

"But what struck me especially was the odor. It was a sickening and perfumed odor, reminding one of rice powder and the mouldy smell of a cellar. An indefinable odor in a heavy atmosphere as oppressive as that of public baths. I followed the maid up a marble stairway, covered with a green, Oriental carpet, and was ushered into a sumptubus parlor.

"Left alone, I looked about me.

"The room was richly furnished, but in the pretentious taste of a parvenu. Rather fine engravings of the last century represented women with powdered hair dressed high surprised by gentlemen in interesting positions. Another lady, lying in a large bed, was teasing with her foot a little dog, lost in the sheets. One drawing showed four feet, bodies concealed behind a curtain. The large room, surrounded by soft couches, was entirely impregnated with that enervating and insipid odor which I had already noticed. There seemed to be something suspicious about the walls, the hangings, the exaggerated luxury, everything.

"I approached the window to look into the garden. It was very big, shady, beautiful. A wide path wound round a grass plot in the midst of which was a fountain, entered a shrubbery and came out farther away. And, suddenly, yonder, in the distance, between two clumps of bushes, three women appeared. They were walking slowly, arm in arm, clad in long, white tea-gowns covered with lace. Two were blondes and the other was dark-haired. Almost immediately they disappeared again behind the trees. I stood there entranced, delighted with this short and charming apparition, which brought to my mind a whole world of poetry. They had scarcely allowed themselves to be seen, in just the proper light, in that frame of foliage, in the midst of that mysterious, delightful park. It seemed to me that I had suddenly seen before me the great ladies of the last century, who were depicted in the engravings on the wall. And I began to think of the happy, joyous, witty and amorous times when manners were so graceful and lips so approachable.

"A deep voice made me jump. Patience had come in, beaming, and held out his hands to me.

"He looked into my eyes with the sly look which one takes when divulging secrets of love, and, with a Napoleonic gesture, he showed me his sumptuous parlor, his park, the three women, who had reappeared in the back of it, then, in a triumphant voice, where the note of pride was prominent, he said:

"'And to think that I began with nothing—my wife and my sister-in-law!'"

ABANDONED

*J*really think you must be mad, my dear, to go for a country walk in such weather as this. You have had some very strange notions for the last two months. You drag me to the seaside in spite of myself, when you have never once had such a whim during all the forty-four years that we have been married. You chose Fecamp, which is a very dull town, without consulting me in the matter, and now you are seized with such a rage for walking, you who hardly ever stir out on foot, that you want to take a country walk on the hottest day of the year. Ask d'Apreval to go with you, as he is ready to gratify all your whims. As for me, I am going back to have a nap."

Madame de Cadour turned to her old friend and said:

"Will you come with me, Monsieur d'Apreval?"

He bowed with a smile, and with all the gallantry of former years:

"I will go wherever you go," he replied.

"Very well, then, go and get a sunstroke," Monsieur de Cadour said; and he went back to the Hotel des Bains to lie down for an hour or two.

As soon as they were alone, the old lady and her old companion set off, and she said to him in a low voice, squeezing his hand:

"At last! at last!"

"You are mad," he said in a whisper. "I assure you that you are mad. Think of the risk you are running. If that man—"

She started.

"Oh! Henri, do not say that man, when you are speaking of him."

"Very well," he said abruptly, "if our son guesses anything, if he has any suspicions, he will have you, he will have us both in his power. You have got on without seeing him for the last forty years. What is the matter with you to-day?"

They had been going up the long street that leads from the sea to the town, and now they turned to the right, to go to Etretat. The white road stretched in front of him, then under a blaze of brilliant sunshine, so they went on slowly in the burning heat. She had taken her old friend's arm, and was looking straight in front of her, with a fixed and haunted gaze, and at last she said:

"And so you have not seen him again, either?"

"No, never."

"Is it possible?"

"My dear friend, do not let us begin that discussion again. I have a wife and children and you have a husband, so we both of us have much to fear from other people's opinion."

She did not reply; she was thinking of her long past youth and of many sad things that had occurred. How well she recalled all the details of their early friendship, his smiles, the way he used to linger, in order to watch her until she was indoors. What happy days they were, the only really delicious days she had ever enjoyed, and how quickly they were over!

And then—her discovery—of the penalty she paid! What anguish!

Of that journey to the South, that long journey, her sufferings, her constant terror, that secluded life in the small, solitary house on the shores of the Mediterranean, at the bottom of a garden, which she did not venture to leave. How well she remembered those long days which she spent lying under an orange tree, looking up at the round, red fruit, amid the green leaves. How she used to long to go out, as far as the sea, whose fresh breezes came to her over the wall, and whose small waves she could hear lapping on the beach. She dreamed of its immense blue expanse sparkling under the sun, with the white sails of the small vessels, and a mountain on the horizon. But she did not dare to go outside the gate. Suppose anybody had recognized her!

And those days of waiting, those last days of misery and expectation! The impending suffering, and then that terrible night! What misery she had endured, and what a night it was! How she had groaned and screamed! She could still see the pale face of her lover, who kissed her hand every moment, and the clean-shaven face of the doctor and the nurse's white cap.

And what she felt when she heard the child's feeble cries, that wail, that first effort of a human's voice!

And the next day! the next day! the only day of her life on which she had seen and kissed her son; for, from that time, she had never even caught a glimpse of him.

And what a long, void existence hers had been since then, with the thought of that child always, always floating before her. She had never seen her son, that little creature that had been part of herself, even once since then; they had taken him from her, carried him away, and had hidden him. All she knew was that he had been brought up by some peasants in Normandy, that he had become a peasant himself, had married well, and that his father, whose name he did not know, had settled a handsome sum of money on him.

How often during the last forty years had she wished to go and see him and to embrace him! She could not imagine to herself that he had grown! She always thought of that small human atom which she had held in her arms and pressed to her bosom for a day.

How often she had said to M. d'Apreval: "I cannot bear it any longer; I must go and see him."

But he had always stopped her and kept her from going. She would be unable to restrain and to master herself; their son would guess it and take advantage of her, blackmail her; she would be lost.

"What is he like?" she said.

"I do not know. I have not seen him again, either."

"Is it possible? To have a son and not to know him; to be afraid of him and to reject him as if he were a disgrace! It is horrible."

They went along the dusty road, overcome by the scorching sun, and continually ascending that interminable hill.

"One might take it for a punishment," she continued; "I have never had another child, and I could no longer resist the longing to see him, which has possessed me for forty years. You men cannot understand that. You must remember that I shall not live much longer, and suppose I should never see him, never have seen him! . . . Is it possible? How could I wait so long? I have thought about him every day since, and what a terrible existence mine has been! I have never awakened, never, do you understand, without my first thoughts being of him, of my child. How is he? Oh, how guilty I feel toward him! Ought one to fear what the world may say in a case like this? I ought to have left everything to go after him, to bring him up and to show my love for him. I should certainly have been much happier, but I did not dare, I was a coward. How I have suffered! Oh, how those poor, abandoned children must hate their mothers!"

She stopped suddenly, for she was choked by her sobs. The whole valley was deserted and silent in the dazzling light and the overwhelming heat, and only the grasshoppers uttered their shrill, continuous chirp among the sparse yellow grass on both sides of the road.

"Sit down a little," he said.

She allowed herself to be led to the side of the ditch and sank down with her face in her hands. Her white hair, which hung in curls on both sides of her face, had become tangled. She wept, overcome by profound grief, while he stood facing her, uneasy and not knowing what to say, and he merely murmured: "Come, take courage."

She got up.

"I will," she said, and wiping her eyes, she began to walk again with the uncertain step of an elderly woman.

A little farther on the road passed beneath a clump of trees, which hid a few houses, and they could distinguish the vibrating and regular blows of a blacksmith's hammer on the anvil; and presently they saw a wagon standing on the right side of the road in front of a low cottage, and two men shoeing a horse under a shed.

Monsieur d'Apreval went up to them.

"Where is Pierre Benedict's farm?" he asked.

"Take the road to the left, close to the inn, and then go straight on; it is the third house past Poret's. There is a small spruce fir close to the gate; you cannot make a mistake."

They turned to the left. She was walking very slowly now, her legs threatened to give way, and her heart was beating so violently that she felt as if she should suffocate, while at every step she murmured, as if in prayer:

"Oh! Heaven! Heaven!"

Monsieur d'Apreval, who was also nervous and rather pale, said to her somewhat gruffly:

"If you cannot manage to control your feelings, you will betray yourself at once. Do try and restrain yourself."

"How can I?" she replied. "My child! When I think that I am going to see my child."

They were going along one of those narrow country lanes between farmyards, that are concealed beneath a double row of beech trees at either side of the ditches, and suddenly they found themselves in front of a gate, beside which there was a young spruce fir.

"This is it," he said.

She stopped suddenly and looked about her. The courtyard, which was planted with apple trees, was large and extended as far as the small thatched dwelling house. On the opposite side were the stable, the barn, the cow house and the poultry house, while the gig, the wagon and the manure cart were under a slated outhouse. Four calves were grazing under the shade of the trees and black hens were wandering all about the enclosure.

All was perfectly still; the house door was open, but nobody was to be seen, and so they went in, when immediately a large black dog came out of a barrel that was standing under a pear tree, and began to bark furiously.

There were four bee-hives on boards against the wall of the house.

Monsieur d'Apreval stood outside and called out:

"Is anybody at home?"

Then a child appeared, a little girl of about ten, dressed in a chemise and a linen, petticoat, with dirty, bare legs and a timid and cunning look. She remained standing in the doorway, as if to prevent any one going in.

"What do you want?" she asked.

"Is your father in?"

"No."

"Where is he?"

"I don't know."

"And your mother?"

"Gone after the cows."

"Will she be back soon?"

"I don't know."

Then suddenly the lady, as if she feared that her companion might force her to return, said quickly:

"I shall not go without having seen him."

"We will wait for him, my dear friend."

As they turned away, they saw a peasant woman coming toward the house, carrying two tin pails, which appeared to be heavy and which glistened brightly in the sunlight.

She limped with her right leg, and in her brown knitted jacket, that was faded by the sun and washed out by the rain, she looked like a poor, wretched, dirty servant.

"Here is mamma," the child said.

When she got close to the house, she looked at the strangers angrily and suspiciously, and then she went in, as if she had not seen them. She looked old and had a hard, yellow, wrinkled face, one of those wooden faces that country people so often have.

Monsieur d'Apreval called her back.

"I beg your pardon, madame, but we came in to know whether you could sell us two glasses of milk."

She was grumbling when she reappeared in the door, after putting down her pails.

"I don't sell milk," she replied.

"We are very thirsty," he said, "and madame is very tired. Can we not get something to drink?"

The peasant woman gave them an uneasy and cunning glance and then she made up her mind.

"As you are here, I will give you some," she said, going into the house, and almost immediately the child came out and brought two chairs, which she placed under an apple tree, and then the mother, in turn, brought out two bowls of foaming milk, which she gave to the visitors. She did not return to the house, however, but remained standing near them, as if to watch them and to find out for what purpose they had come there.

"You have come from Fecamp?" she said.

"Yes," Monsieur d'Apreval replied, "we are staying at Fecamp for the summer."

And then, after a short silence, he continued:

"Have you any fowls you could sell us every week?"

The woman hesitated for a moment and then replied:

"Yes, I think I have. I suppose you want young ones?"

"Yes, of course."

"What do you pay for them in the market?"

D'Apreval, who had not the least idea, turned to his companion: "What are you paying for poultry in Fecamp, my dear lady?"

"Four francs and four francs fifty centimes," she said, her eyes full of tears, while the farmer's wife, who was looking at her askance, asked in much surprise:

"Is the lady ill, as she is crying?"

He did not know what to say, and replied with some hesitation:

"No—no—but she lost her watch as we came along, a very handsome watch, and that troubles her. If anybody should find it, please let us know."

Mother Benedict did not reply, as she thought it a very equivocal sort of answer, but suddenly she exclaimed:

"Oh, here is my husband!"

She was the only one who had seen him, as she was facing the gate. D'Apreval started and Madame de Cadour nearly fell as she turned round suddenly on her chair.

A man bent nearly double, and out of breath, stood there, ten-yards from them, dragging a cow at the end of a rope. Without taking any notice of the visitors, he said:

"Confound it! What a brute!"

And he went past them and disappeared in the cow house.

Her tears had dried quickly as she sat there startled, without a word and with the one thought in her mind, that this was her son, and D'Apreval, whom the same thought had struck very unpleasantly, said in an agitated voice:

"Is this Monsieur Benedict?"

"Who told you his name?" the wife asked, still rather suspiciously.

"The blacksmith at the corner of the highroad," he replied, and then they were all silent, with their eyes fixed on the door of the cow house, which formed a sort of black hole in the wall of the building. Nothing could be seen inside, but they heard a vague noise, movements and footsteps and the sound of hoofs, which were deadened by the straw on the floor, and soon the man reappeared in the door, wiping his forehead, and came toward the house with long, slow strides. He passed the strangers without seeming to notice them and said to his wife:

"Go and draw me a jug of cider; I am very thirsty."

Then he went back into the house, while his wife went into the cellar and left the two Parisians alone.

"Let us go, let us go, Henri," Madame de Cadour said, nearly distracted with grief, and so d'Apreval took her by the arm, helped her to rise, and sustaining her with all his strength, for he felt that she was nearly fainting, he led her out, after throwing five francs on one of the chairs.

As soon as they were outside the gate, she began to sob and said, shaking with grief:

"Oh! oh! is that what you have made of him?"

He was very pale and replied coldly:

"I did what I could. His farm is worth eighty thousand francs, and that is more than most of the sons of the middle classes have."

They returned slowly, without speaking a word. She was still crying; the tears ran down her cheeks continually for a time, but by degrees they stopped, and they went back to Fecamp, where they found Monsieur de Cadour waiting dinner for them. As soon as he saw them, he began to laugh and exclaimed:

"So my wife has had a sunstroke, and I am very glad of it. I really think she has lost her head for some time past!"

Neither of them replied, and when the husband asked them, rubbing his hands:

"Well, I hope that, at least, you have had a pleasant walk?"

Monsieur d'Apreval replied:

"A delightful walk, I assure you; perfectly delightful."

THE MAISON TELLIER

PART I

They went there every evening about eleven o'clock, just as they would go to the club. Six or eight of them; always the same set, not fast men, but respectable tradesmen, and young men in government or some other employ, and they would drink their Chartreuse, and laugh with the girls, or else talk seriously with Madame Tellier, whom everybody respected, and then they would go home at twelve o'clock! The younger men would sometimes stay later.

It was a small, comfortable house painted yellow, at the corner of a street behind Saint Etienne's Church, and from the windows one could see the docks full of ships being unloaded, the big salt marsh, and, rising beyond it, the Virgin's Hill with its old gray chapel.

Madame Tellier, who came of a respectable family of peasant proprietors in the Department of the Eure, had taken up her profession, just as she would have become a milliner or dressmaker. The prejudice which is so violent and deeply rooted in large towns, does not exist in the country places in Normandy. The peasant says:

"It is a paying-business," and he sends his daughter to keep an establishment of this character just as he would send her to keep a girls' school.

She had inherited the house from an old uncle, to whom it had belonged. Monsieur and Madame Tellier, who had formerly been innkeepers near Yvetot, had immediately sold their house, as they thought that the business at Fecamp was more profitable, and they arrived one fine morning to assume the direction of the enterprise, which was declining on account of the absence of the proprietors. They were good people enough in their way, and soon made themselves liked by their staff and their neighbors.

Monsieur died of apoplexy two years later, for as the new place kept him in idleness and without any exercise, he had grown excessively stout, and his health had suffered. Since she had been a widow, all the frequenters of the establishment made much of her; but people said that, personally, she was quite virtuous, and even the girls in the house could not discover anything against her. She was tall, stout and affable, and her complexion, which had become pale in the dimness of her house, the shutters of which were scarcely ever opened, shone as if it had been varnished. She had a fringe of curly false hair, which gave her a juvenile look, that contrasted strongly with the ripeness of her figure. She was always smiling and cheerful, and was fond of a joke, but there was a shade of reserve about her, which her occupation had not quite made her lose. Coarse words always shocked her, and when any young fellow who had been badly brought up called her establishment a hard name, she was angry and disgusted.

In a word, she had a refined mind, and although she treated her women as friends, yet she very frequently used to say that "she and they were not made of the same stuff."

Sometimes during the week she would hire a carriage and take some of her girls into the country, where they used to enjoy themselves on the grass by the side of the little river. They were like a lot of girls let out from school, and would run races and play childish games. They had a cold dinner on the grass, and drank cider, and went home at night with a delicious feeling of fatigue, and in the carriage they kissed Madame' Tellier as their kind mother, who was full of goodness and complaisance.

The house had two entrances. At the corner there was a sort of tap-room, which sailors and the lower orders frequented at night, and she had two girls whose special duty it was to wait on them with the assistance of Frederic, a short, light-haired, beardless fellow, as strong as a horse. They set the half bottles of wine and the jugs of beer on the shaky marble tables before the customers, and then urged the men to drink.

The three other girls—there were only five of them—formed a kind of aristocracy, and they remained with the company on the first floor, unless they were wanted downstairs and there was nobody on the first floor. The salon de Jupiter, where the tradesmen used to meet, was papered in blue, and embellished with a large drawing representing Leda and the swan. The room was reached by a winding staircase, through a narrow door opening on the street, and above this door a lantern inclosed in wire, such as one still sees in some towns, at the foot of the shrine of some saint, burned all night long.

The house, which was old and damp, smelled slightly of mildew. At times there was an odor of eau de Cologne in the passages, or sometimes from a half-open door downstairs the noisy mirth of the common men sitting and drinking rose to the first floor, much to the disgust of the gentlemen who were there. Madame Tellier, who was on friendly terms with her customers, did not leave the room, and took much interest in what was going on in the town, and they regularly told her all the news. Her serious conversation was a change from the ceaseless chatter of the three women; it was a rest from the obscene jokes of those stout individuals who every evening indulged in the commonplace debauchery of drinking a glass of liqueur in company with common women.

The names of the girls on the first floor were Fernande, Raphaele, and Rosa, the Jade. As the staff was limited, madame had endeavored that each member of it should be a pattern, an epitome of the feminine type, so that every customer might find as nearly as possible the realization of his ideal. Fernande represented the handsome blonde; she was very tall, rather fat, and lazy; a country girl, who could not get rid of her freckles, and whose short, light, almost colorless, tow-like hair, like combed-out hemp, barely covered her head.

Raphaele, who came from Marseilles, played the indispensable part of the handsome Jewess, and was thin, with high cheekbones, which were covered with rouge, and black hair covered with pomatum, which curled on her forehead. Her eyes would have been handsome, if the right one had not had a speck in it. Her Roman nose came down over a square jaw, where two false upper teeth contrasted strangely with the bad color of the rest.

Rosa was a little roll of fat, nearly all body, with very short legs, and from morning till night she sang songs, which were alternately risque or sentimental, in a harsh voice; told silly, interminable tales, and only stopped talking in order to eat, and left off eating in order to talk; she was never still, and was active as a squirrel, in spite of her embonpoint and her short legs; her laugh, which was a torrent of shrill cries, resounded here and there, ceaselessly, in a bedroom, in the loft, in the cafe, everywhere, and all about nothing.

The two women on the ground floor, Lodise, who was nicknamed La Cocotte, and Flora, whom they called Balancoise, because she limped a little, the former always dressed as the Goddess of Liberty, with a tri-colored sash, and the other as a Spanish woman, with a string of copper coins in her carroty hair, which jingled at every uneven step, looked like cooks dressed up for the carnival. They were like all other women of the lower orders, neither uglier nor better looking than they usually are.

They looked just like servants at an inn, and were generally called "the two pumps."

A jealous peace, which was, however, very rarely disturbed, reigned among these five women, thanks to Madame Tellier's conciliatory wisdom, and to her constant good humor, and the establishment, which was the only one of the kind in the little town, was very much frequented. Madame Tellier had succeeded in giving it such a respectable appearance, she was so amiable and obliging to everybody, her good heart was so well known, that she was treated with a certain amount of consideration. The regular customers spent money on her, and were delighted when she was especially friendly toward them, and when they met during the day, they would say: "Until this evening, you know where," just as men say: "At the club, after dinner." In a word, Madame Tellier's house was somewhere to go to, and they very rarely missed their daily meetings there.

One evening toward the end of May, the first arrival, Monsieur Poulin, who was a timber merchant, and had been mayor, found the door shut. The lantern behind the grating was not alight; there was not a sound in the house; everything seemed dead. He knocked, gently at first, but then more loudly, but nobody answered the door. Then he went slowly up the street, and when he got to the market place he met Monsieur Duvert, the gunmaker, who was going to the same place, so they went back together, but did not meet with any better success. But suddenly they heard a loud noise, close to them, and on going round the house, they saw a number of English and French sailors, who were hammering at the closed shutters of the taproom with their fists.

The two tradesmen immediately made their escape, but a low "Pst!" stopped them; it was Monsieur Tournevau, the fish curer, who had recognized them, and was trying to attract their attention. They told him what had happened, and he was all the more annoyed, as he was a married man and father of a family, and only went on Saturdays. That was his regular evening, and now he should be deprived of this dissipation for the whole week.

The three men went as far as the quay together, and on the way they met young Monsieur Philippe, the banker's son, who frequented the place regularly, and Monsieur Pinipesse, the collector, and they all returned to the Rue aux Juifs together, to make a last attempt. But the exasperated sailors were besieging the house, throwing stones at the shutters, and shouting, and the five first-floor customers went away as quickly as possible, and walked aimlessly about the streets.

Presently they met Monsieur Dupuis, the insurance agent, and then Monsieur Vasse, the Judge of the Tribunal of Commerce, and they took a long walk, going to the pier first of all, where they sat down in a row on the granite parapet and watched the rising tide, and when the promenaders had sat there for some time, Monsieur Tournevau said:

"This is not very amusing!"

"Decidedly not," Monsieur Pinipesse replied, and they started off to walk again.

After going through the street alongside the hill, they returned over the wooden bridge which crosses the Retenue, passed close to the railway, and came out again on the market place, when, suddenly, a quarrel arose between Monsieur Pinipesse, the collector, and Monsieur Tournevau about an edible mushroom which one of them declared he had found in the neighborhood.

As they were out of temper already from having nothing to do, they would very probably have come to blows, if the others had not interfered. Monsieur Pinipesse went off furious, and soon another altercation arose between the ex-mayor, Monsieur Poulin, and Monsieur Dupuis, the insurance agent, on the subject of the tax collector's salary and the profits which he might make. Insulting remarks were freely passing between them, when a torrent of formidable cries was heard, and the body of sailors, who were tired of waiting so long outside a closed house, came into the square. They were walking arm in arm, two and two, and formed a long procession, and were shouting furiously. The townsmen hid themselves in a doorway, and the yelling crew disappeared in the direction of the abbey. For a long time they still heard the noise, which diminished like a storm in the distance, and then silence was restored. Monsieur Poulin and Monsieur Dupuis, who were angry with each other, went in different directions, without wishing each other good-by.

The other four set off again, and instinctively went in the direction of Madame Tellier's establishment, which was still closed, silent, impenetrable. A quiet, but obstinate drunken man was knocking at the door of the lower room, antd then stopped and called Frederic, in a low voice, but finding that he got no answer, he sat down on the doorstep, and waited the course of events.

The others were just going to retire, when the noisy band of sailors reappeared at the end of the street. The French sailors were shouting the "Marseillaise," and the Englishmen "Rule Britannia." There was a general lurching against the wall, and then the drunken fellows went on their way toward the quay, where a fight broke out between the two nations, in the course of which an Englishman had his arm broken and a Frenchman his nose split.

The drunken man who had waited outside the door, was crying by that time, as drunken men and children cry when they are vexed, and the others went away. By degrees, calm was restored in the noisy town; here and there, at moments, the distant sound of voices could be heard, and then died away in the distance.

One man only was still wandering about, Monsieur Tournevau, the fish curer, who was annoyed at having to wait until the following Saturday, and he hoped something would turn up, he did not know what; but he was exasperated at the police for thus allowing an establishment of such public utility, which they had under their control, to be closed.

He went back to it and examined the walls, trying to find out some reason, and on the shutter he saw a notice stuck up. He struck a wax match and read the following, in a large, uneven hand: "Closed on account of the Confirmation."

Then he went away, as he saw it was useless to remain, and left the drunken man lying on the pavement fast asleep, outside that inhospitable door.

The next day, all the regular customers, one after the other, found some reason for going through the street, with a bundle of papers under their arm to keep them in countenance, and with a furtive glance they all read that mysterious notice:

"Closed on account of the Confirmation."

PART II

Madame Tellier had a brother, who was a carpenter in their native place, Virville, in the Department of Eure. When she still kept the inn at Yvetot, she had stood godmother to that brother's daughter, who had received the name of Constance—Constance Rivet; she herself being a Rivet on her father's side. The carpenter, who knew that his sister was in a good position, did not lose sight of her, although they did not meet often, for they were both kept at home by their occupations, and lived a long way from each other. But as the girl was twelve years old, and going to be confirmed, he seized that opportunity to write to his sister, asking her to come and be present at the ceremony. Their old parents were dead, and as she could not well refuse her goddaughter, she accepted the invitation. Her brother, whose name was Joseph, hoped that by dint of showing his sister attention, she might be induced to make her will in the girl's favor, as she had no children of her own.

His sister's occupation did not trouble his scruples in the least, and, besides, nobody knew anything about it at Virville. When they spoke of her, they only said: "Madame Tellier is living at Fecamp," which might mean that she was living on her own private income. It was quite twenty leagues from Fecamp to Virville, and for a peasant, twenty leagues on land is as long a journey as crossing the ocean would be to city people. The people at Virville had never been further than Rouen, and nothing attracted the people from Fecamp to a village of five hundred houses in the middle of a plain, and situated in another department; at any rate, nothing was known about her business.

But the Confirmation was coming on, and Madame Tellier was in great embarrassment. She had no substitute, and did not at all care to leave her house, even for a day; for all the rivalries between the girls upstairs and those downstairs would infallibly break out. No doubt Frederic would get drunk, and when he was in that state, he would knock anybody down for a mere word. At last, however, she made up her mind to take them all with her, with the exception of the man, to whom she gave a holiday until the next day but one.

When she asked her brother, he made no objection, but undertook to put them all up for a night, and so on Saturday morning the eight-o'clock express carried off Madame Tellier and her companions in a second-class carriage. As far as Beuzeville they were alone, and chattered like magpies, but at that station a couple got in. The man, an old peasant, dressed in a blue blouse with a turned-down collar, wide sleeves tight at the wrist, ornamented with white embroidery, wearing an old high hat with long nap, held an enormous green umbrella in one hand, and a large basket in the other, from which the heads of three frightened ducks protruded. The woman, who sat up stiffly in her rustic finery, had a face like a fowl, with a nose that was as pointed as a bill. She sat down opposite her husband and did not stir, as she was startled at finding herself in such smart company.

There was certainly an array of striking colors in the carriage. Madame Tellier was dressed in blue silk from head to foot, and had on a dazzling red imitation French cashmere shawl. Fernande was puffing in a Scotch plaid dress, of which her companions had laced the bodice as tight as they could, forcing up her full bust, that was continually heaving up and down. Raphaele, with a bonnet covered with feathers, so that it looked like a bird's nest, had on a lilac dress with gold spots on it, and there was something Oriental about it that suited her Jewish face. Rosa had on a pink skirt with largo flounces, and looked like a very fat child, an obese dwarf; while the two Pumps looked as if they had cut their dresses out of old flowered curtains dating from the Restoration.

As soon as they were no longer alone in the compartment, the ladies put on staid looks, and began to talk of subjects which might give others a high opinion of them. But at Bolbeck a gentleman with light whiskers, a gold chain, and wearing two or three rings, got in, and put several parcels wrapped in oilcloth on the rack over his head. He looked inclined for a joke, and seemed a good-hearted fellow.

"Are you ladies changing your quarters?" he said, and that question embarrassed them all considerably. Madame Tellier, however, quickly regained her composure, and said sharply, to avenge the honor of her corps:

"I think you might try and be polite!"

He excused himself, and said: "I beg your pardon, I ought to have said your nunnery."

She could not think of a retort, so, perhaps thinking she had said enough, madame gave him a dignified bow and compressed her lips.

Then the gentleman, who was sitting between Rosa and the old peasant, began to wink knowingly at the ducks whose heads were sticking out of the basket, and when he felt that he had fixed the attention of his public, he began to tickle them under the bills and spoke funnily to them to make the company smile.

"We have left our little pond, quack! quack! to make the acquaintance of the little spit, qu-ack! qu-ack!"

The unfortunate creatures turned their necks away, to avoid his caresses, and made desperate efforts to get out of their wicker prison, and then, suddenly, all at once, uttered the most lamentable quacks of distress. The women exploded with laughter. They leaned forward and pushed each other, so as to see better; they were very much interested in the ducks, and the gentleman redoubled his airs, his wit and his teasing.

Rosa joined in, and leaning over her neighbor's legs, she kissed the three animals on the head, and immediately all the girls wanted to kiss them, in turn, and as they did so the gentleman took them on his knee, jumped them up and down and pinched their arms. The two peasants, who were even in greater consternation than their poultry, rolled their eyes as if they were possessed, without venturing to move, and their old wrinkled faces had not a smile, not a twitch.

Then the gentleman, who was a commercial traveller, offered the ladies suspenders by way of a joke, and taking up one of his packages, he opened it. It was a joke, for the parcel contained garters. There were blue silk, pink silk, red silk, violet silk, mauve silk garters, and the buckles were made of two gilt metal cupids embracing each other. The girls uttered exclamations of delight and looked at them with that gravity natural to all women when they are considering an article of dress. They consulted one another by their looks or in a whisper, and replied in the same manner, and Madame Tellier was longingly handling a pair of orange garters that were broader and more imposing looking than the rest; really fit for the mistress of such an establishment.

The gentleman waited, for he had an idea.

"Come, my kittens," he said, "you must try them on."

There was a torrent of exclamations, and they squeezed their petticoats between their legs, but he quietly waited his time and said: "Well, if you will not try them on I shall pack them up again."

And he added cunningly: "I offer any pair they like to those who will try them on."

But they would not, and sat up very straight and looked dignified.

But the two Pumps looked so distressed that he renewed his offer to them, and Flora, especially, visibly hesitated, and he insisted: "Come, my dear, a little courage! Just look at that lilac pair; it will suit your dress admirably."

That decided her, and pulling up her dress she showed a thick leg fit for a milkmaid, in a badly fitting, coarse stocking. The commercial traveller stooped down and fastened the garter. When he had done this, he gave her the lilac pair and asked: "Who next?"

"I! I!" they all shouted at once, and he began on Rosa, who uncovered a shapeless, round thing without any ankle, a regular "sausage of a leg," as Raphaele used to say.

Lastly, Madame Tellier herself put out her leg, a handsome, muscular Norman leg, and in his surprise and pleasure, the commercial traveller gallantly took off his hat to salute that master calf, like a true French cavalier.

The two peasants, who were speechless from surprise, glanced sideways out of the corner of one eye, and they looked so exactly like fowls that the man with the light whiskers, when he sat up, said: "Co—co—ri—co" under their very noses, and that gave rise to another storm of amusement.

The old people got out at Motteville with their basket, their ducks and their umbrella, and they heard the woman say to her husband as they went away:

"They are no good and are off to that cursed place, Paris."

The funny commercial traveller himself got out at Rouen, after behaving so coarsely that Madame Tellier was obliged sharply to put him in his right place, and she added, as a moral: "This will teach us not to talk to the first comer."

At Oissel they changed trains, and at a little station further on Monsieur Joseph Rivet was waiting for them with a large cart with a number of chairs in it, drawn by a white horse.

The carpenter politely kissed all the ladies and then helped them into his conveyance.

Three of them sat on three chairs at the back, Raphaele, Madame Tellier and her brother on the three chairs in front, while Rosa, who had no seat, settled herself as comfortably as she could on tall Fernande's knees, and then they set off.

But the horse's jerky trot shook the cart so terribly that the chairs began to dance and threw the travellers about, to the right and to the left, as if they were dancing puppets, which made them scream and make horrible grimaces.

They clung on to the sides of the vehicle, their bonnets fell on their backs, over their faces and on their shoulders, and the white horse went on stretching out his head and holding out his little hairless tail like a rat's, with which he whisked his buttocks from time to time.

Joseph Rivet, with one leg on the shafts and the other doubled under him, held the reins with his elbows very high, and kept uttering a kind of clucking sound, which made the horse prick up its ears and go faster.

The green country extended on either side of the road, and here and there the colza in flower presented a waving expanse of yellow, from which arose a strong, wholesome, sweet and penetrating odor, which the wind carried to some distance.

The cornflowers showed their little blue heads amid the rye, and the women wanted to pick them, but Monsieur Rivet refused to stop.

Then, sometimes, a whole field appeared to be covered with blood, so thick were the poppies, and the cart, which looked as if it were filled with flowers of more brilliant hue, jogged on through fields bright with wild flowers, and disappeared behind the trees of a farm, only to reappear and to go on again through the yellow or green standing crops, which were studded with red or blue.

One o'clock struck as they drove up to the carpenter's door. They were tired out and pale with hunger, as they had eaten nothing since they left home. Madame Rivet ran out and made them alight, one after another, and kissed them as soon as they were on the ground, and she seemed as if she would never tire of kissing her sister-in-law, whom she apparently wanted to monopolize. They had lunch in the workshop, which had been cleared out for the next day's dinner.

The capital omelet, followed by boiled chitterlings and washed down with good hard cider, made them all feel comfortable.

Rivet had taken a glass so that he might drink with them, and his wife cooked, waited on them, brought in the dishes, took them out and asked each of them in a whisper whether they had everything they wanted. A number of boards standing against the walls and heaps of shavings that had been swept into the corners gave out a smell of planed wood, a smell of a carpenter's shop, that resinous odor which penetrates to the lungs.

They wanted to see the little girl, but she had gone to church and would not be back again until evening, so they all went out for a stroll in the country.

It was a small village, through which the highroad passed. Ten or a dozen houses on either side of the single street were inhabited by the butcher, the grocer, the carpenter, the innkeeper, the shoemaker and the baker.

The church was at the end of the street and was surrounded by a small churchyard, and four immense lime-trees, which stood just outside the porch, shaded it completely. It was built of flint, in no particular style, and had a slate-roofed steeple. When you got past it, you were again in the open country, which was varied here and there by clumps of trees which hid the homesteads.

Rivet had given his arm to his sister, out of politeness, although he was in his working clothes, and was walking with her in a dignified manner. His wife, who was overwhelmed by Raphaele's gold-striped dress, walked between her and Fernande, and roly-poly Rosa was trotting behind with Louise and Flora, the Seesaw, who was limping along, quite tired out.

The inhabitants came to their doors, the children left off playing, and a window curtain would be raised, so as to show a muslin cap, while an old woman with a crutch, who was almost blind, crossed herself as if it were a religious procession, and they all gazed for a long time at those handsome ladies from town, who had come so far to be present at the confirmation of Joseph Rivet's little girl, and the carpenter rose very much in the public estimation.

As they passed the church they heard some children singing. Little shrill voices were singing a hymn, but Madame Tellier would not let them go in, for fear of disturbing the little cherubs.

After the walk, during which Joseph Rivet enumerated the principal landed proprietors, spoke about the yield of the land and the productiveness of the cows and sheep, he took his tribe of women home and installed them in his house, and as it was very small, they had to put them into the rooms, two and two.

Just for once Rivet would sleep in the workshop on the shavings; his wife was to share her bed with her sister-in-law, and Fernande and Raphaele were to sleep together in the next room. Louise and Flora were put into the kitchen, where they had a mattress on the floor, and Rosa had a little dark cupboard to herself at the top of the stairs, close to the loft, where the candidate for confirmation was to sleep.

When the little girl came in she was overwhelmed with kisses; all the women wished to caress her with that need of tender expansion, that habit of professional affection which had made them kiss the ducks in the railway carriage.

They each of them took her on their knees, stroked her soft, light hair and pressed her in their arms with vehement and spontaneous outbursts of affection, and the child, who was very good and religious, bore it all patiently.

As the day had been a fatiguing one for everybody, they all went to bed soon after dinner. The whole village was wrapped in that perfect stillness of the country, which is almost like a religious silence, and the girls, who were accustomed to the noisy evenings of their establishment, felt rather impressed by the perfect repose of the sleeping village, and they shivered, not with cold, but with those little shivers of loneliness which come over uneasy and troubled hearts.

As soon as they were in bed, two and two together, they clasped each other in their arms, as if to protect themselves against this feeling of the calm and profound slumber of the earth. But Rosa, who was alone in her little dark cupboard, felt a vague and painful emotion come over her.

She was tossing about in bed, unable to get to sleep, when she heard the faint sobs of a crying child close to her head, through the partition. She was frightened, and called out, and was answered by a weak voice, broken by sobs. It was the little girl, who was always used to sleeping in her mother's room, and who was afraid in her small attic.

Rosa was delighted, got up softly so as not to awaken any one, and went and fetched the child. She took her into her warm bed, kissed her and pressed her to her bosom, lavished exaggerated manifestations of tenderness on her, and at last grew calmer herself and went to sleep. And till morning the candidate for confirmation slept with her head on Rosa's bosom.

At five o'clock the little church bell, ringing the Angelus, woke the women, who usually slept the whole morning long.

The villagers were up already, and the women went busily from house to house, carefully bringing short, starched muslin dresses or very long wax tapers tied in the middle with a bow of silk fringed with gold, and with dents in the wax for the fingers.

The sun was already high in the blue sky, which still had a rosy tint toward the horizon, like a faint remaining trace of dawn. Families of fowls were walking about outside the houses, and here and there a black cock, with a glistening breast, raised his head, which was crowned by his red comb, flapped his wings and uttered his shrill crow, which the other cocks repeated.

Vehicles of all sorts came from neighboring parishes, stopping at the different houses, and tall Norman women dismounted, wearing dark dresses, with kerchiefs crossed over the bosom, fastened with silver brooches a hundred years old.

The men had put on their blue smocks over their new frock-coats or over their old dress-coats of green-cloth, the two tails of which hung down below their blouses. When the horses were in the stable there was a double line of rustic conveyances along the road: carts, cabriolets, tilburies, wagonettes, traps of every shape and age, tipping forward on their shafts or else tipping backward with the shafts up in the air.

The carpenter's house was as busy as a bee-hive. The women, in dressing-jackets and petticoats, with their thin, short hair, which looked faded and worn, hanging down their backs, were busy dressing the child, who was standing quietly on a table, while Madame Tellier was directing the movements of her battalion. They washed her, did her hair, dressed her, and with the help of a number of pins, they arranged the folds of her dress and took in the waist, which was too large.

Then, when she was ready, she was told to sit down and not to move, and the women hurried off to get ready themselves.

The church bell began to ring again, and its tinkle was lost in the air, like a feeble voice which is soon drowned in space. The candidates came out of the houses and went toward the parochial building, which contained the two schools and the mansion house, and which stood quite at one end of the village, while the church was situated at the other.

The parents, in their very best clothes, followed their children, with embarrassed looks, and those clumsy movements of a body bent by toil.

The little girls disappeared in a cloud of muslin, which looked like whipped cream, while the lads, who looked like embryo waiters in a cafe and whose heads shone with pomatum, walked with their legs apart, so as not to get any dust or dirt on their black trousers.

It was something for a family, to be proud of, when a large number of relatives, who had come from a distance, surrounded the child, and the carpenter's triumph was complete.

Madame Tellier's regiment, with its leader at its head, followed Constance; her father gave his arm to his sister, her mother walked by the side of Raphaele, Fernande with Rosa and Louise and Flora together, and thus they proceeded majestically through the village, like a general's staff in full uniform, while the effect on the village was startling.

At the school the girls ranged themselves under the Sister of Mercy and the boys under the schoolmaster, and they started off, singing a hymn as they went. The boys led the way, in two files, between the two rows of vehicles, from which the horses had been taken out, and the girls followed in the same order; and as all the people in the village had given the town ladies the precedence out of politeness, they came immediately behind the girls, and lengthened the double line of the procession still more, three on the right and three on the left, while their dresses were as striking as a display of fireworks.

When they went into the church the congregation grew quite excited. They pressed against each other, turned round and jostled one another in order to see, and some of the devout ones spoke almost aloud, for they were so astonished at the sight of those ladies whose dresses were more elaborate than the priest's vestments.

The mayor offered them his pew, the first one on the right, close to the choir, and Madame Tellier sat there with her sister-in-law, Fernande and Raphaele. Rosa, Louise and Flora occupied the second seat, in company with the carpenter.

The choir was full of kneeling children, the girls on one side and the boys on the other, and the long wax tapers which they held looked like lances pointing in all directions, and three men were standing in front of the lectern, singing as loud as they could.

They prolonged the syllables of the sonorous Latin indefinitely, holding on to "Amens" with interminable "a-a's," which the reed stop of the organ sustained in a monotonous, long-drawn-out tone.

A child's shrill voice took up the reply, and from time to time a priest sitting in a stall and wearing a biretta got up, muttered something and sat down again, while the three singers continued, their eyes fixed on the big book of plain chant lying open before them on the outstretched wings of a wooden eagle.

Then silence ensued and the service went on. Toward the close Rosa, with her head in both hands, suddenly thought of her mother, her village church and her first communion. She almost fancied that that day had returned, when she was so small and was almost hidden in her white dress, and she began to cry.

First of all she wept silently, and the tears dropped slowly from her eyes, but her emotion in creased with her recollections, and she began to sob. She took out her pocket handkerchief, wiped her eyes and held it to her mouth, so as not to scream, but it was in vain. A sort of rattle escaped her throat, and she was answered by two other profound, heartbreaking sobs, for her two neighbors, Louise and Flora, who were kneeling near her, overcome by similar recollections, were sobbing by her side, amid a flood of tears; and as tears are contagious, Madame Tellier soon in turn found that her eyes were wet, and on turning to her sister-in-law, she saw that all the occupants of her seat were also crying.

Soon, throughout the church, here and there, a wife, a mother, a sister, seized by the strange sympathy of poignant emotion, and affected at the sight of those handsome ladies on their knees, shaken with sobs was moistening her cambric pocket handkerchief and pressing her beating heart with her left hand.

Just as the sparks from an engine will set fire to dry grass, so the tears of Rosa and of her companions infected the whole congregation in a moment. Men, women, old men and lads in new smocks were soon all sobbing, and something superhuman seemed to be hovering over their heads—a spirit, the powerful breath of an invisible and all powerful Being.

Suddenly a species of madness seemed to pervade the church, the noise of a crowd in a state of frenzy, a tempest of sobs and stifled cries. It came like gusts of wind which blow the trees in a forest, and the priest, paralyzed by emotion, stammered out incoherent prayers, without finding words, ardent prayers of the soul soaring to heaven.

The people behind him gradually grew calmer. The cantors, in all the dignity of their white surplices, went on in somewhat uncertain voices, and the reed stop itself seemed hoarse, as if the instrument had been weeping; the priest, however, raised his hand to command silence and went and stood on the chancel steps, when everybody was silent at once.

After a few remarks on what had just taken place, and which he attributed to a miracle, he continued, turning to the seats where the carpenter's guests were sitting; "I especially thank you, my dear sisters, who have come from such a distance, and whose presence among us, whose evident faith and ardent piety have set such a salutary example to all. You have edified my parish; your emotion has warmed all hearts; without you, this great day would not, perhaps, have had this really divine character. It is sufficient, at times, that there should be one chosen lamb, for the Lord to descend on His flock."

His voice failed him again, from emotion, and he said no more, but concluded the service.

They now left the church as quickly as possible; the children themselves were restless and tired with such a prolonged tension of the mind. The parents left the church by degrees to see about dinner.

There was a crowd outside, a noisy crowd, a babel of loud voices, where the shrill Norman accent was discernible. The villagers formed two ranks, and when the children appeared, each family took possession of their own.

The whole houseful of women caught hold of Constance, surrounded her and kissed her, and Rosa was especially demonstrative. At last she took hold of one hand, while Madame Tellier took the other, and Raphaele and Fernande held up her long muslin skirt, so that it might not drag in the dust; Louise and Flora brought up the rear with Madame Rivet; and the child, who was very silent and thoughtful, set off for home in the midst of this guard of honor.

Dinner was served in the workshop on long boards supported by trestles, and through the open door they could see all the enjoyment that was going on in the village. Everywhere they were feasting, and through every window were to be seen tables surrounded by people in their Sunday best, and a cheerful noise was heard in every house, while the men sat in their shirt-sleeves, drinking glass after glass of cider.

In the carpenter's house the gaiety maintained somewhat of an air of reserve, the consequence of the emotion of the girls in the morning, and Rivet was the only one who was in a jolly mood, and he was drinking to excess. Madame Tellier looked at the clock every moment, for, in order not to lose two days running, they must take the 3:55 train, which would bring them to Fecamp by dark.

The carpenter tried very hard to distract her attention, so as to keep his guests until the next day, but he did not succeed, for she never joked when there was business on hand, and as soon as they had had their coffee she ordered her girls to make haste and get ready, and then, turning to her brother, she said:

"You must put in the horse immediately," and she herself went to finish her last preparations.

When she came down again, her sister-in-law was waiting to speak to her about the child, and a long conversation took place, in which, however, nothing was settled. The carpenter's wife was artful and pretended to be very much affected, and Madame Tellier, who was holding the girl on her knee, would not pledge herself to anything definite, but merely gave vague promises—she would not forget her, there was plenty of time, and besides, they would meet again.

But the conveyance did not come to the door and the women did not come downstairs. Upstairs they even heard loud laughter, romping, little screams, and much clapping of hands, and so, while the carpenter's wife went to the stable to see whether the cart was ready, madame went upstairs.

Rivet, who was very drunk, was plaguing Rosa, who was half choking with laughter. Louise and Flora were holding him by the arms and trying to calm him, as they were shocked at his levity after that morning's ceremony; but Raphaele and Fernande were urging him on, writhing and holding their sides with laughter, and they uttered shrill cries at every rebuff the drunken fellow received.

The man was furious, his face was red, and he was trying to shake off the two women who were clinging to him, while he was pulling Rosa's skirt with all his might and stammering incoherently.

But Madame Tellier, who was very indignant, went up to her brother, seized him by the shoulders, and threw him out of the room with such violence that he fell against the wall in the passage, and a minute afterward they heard him pumping water on his head in the yard, and when he reappeared with the cart he was quite calm.

They started off in the same way as they had come the day before, and the little white horse started off with his quick, dancing trot. Under the hot sun, their fun, which had been checked during dinner, broke out again. The girls now were amused at the jolting of the cart, pushed their neighbors' chairs, and burst out laughing every moment.

There was a glare of light over the country, which dazzled their eyes, and the wheels raised two trails of dust along the highroad. Presently, Fernande, who was fond of music, asked Rosa to sing something, and she boldly struck up the "Gros Cure de Meudon," but Madame Tellier made her stop immediately, as she thought it a very unsuitable song for such a day, and she added:

"Sing us something of Beranger's." And so, after a moment's hesitation, Rosa began Beranger's song "The Grandmother" in her worn-out voice, and all the girls, and even Madame Tellier herself, joined in the chorus:

> "How I regret
> My dimpled arms,
> My nimble legs,
> And vanished charms."

"That is first rate," Rivet declared, carried away by the rhythm, and they shouted the refrain to every verse, while Rivet beat time on the shaft with his foot, and with the reins on the back of the horse, who, as if he himself were carried away by the rhythm, broke into a wild gallop, and threw all the women in a heap, one on top of the other, on the bottom of the conveyance.

They got up, laughing as if they were mad, and the Gong went on, shouted at the top of their voices, beneath the burning sky, among the ripening grain, to the rapid gallop of the little horse, who set off every time the refrain was sung, and galloped a hundred yards, to their great delight, while occasionally a stone-breaker by the roadside sat up and looked at the load of shouting females through his wire spectacles.

When they got out at the station, the carpenter said: "I am sorry you are going; we might have had some good times together." But Madame Tellier replied very sensibly: "Everything has its right time, and we cannot always be enjoying ourselves." And then he had a sudden inspiration:

"Look here, I will come and see you at Fecamp next month."

And he gave Rosa a roguish and knowing look.

"Come," his sister replied, "you must be sensible; you may come if you like, but you are not to be up to any of your tricks."

He did not reply, and as they heard the whistle of the train, he immediately began to kiss them all. When it came to Rosa's turn, he tried to get to her mouth, which she, however, smiling with her lips closed, turned away from him each time by a rapid movement of her head to one side. He held her in his arms, but he could not attain his object, as his large whip, which he was holding in his hand and waving behind the girl's back in desperation, interfered with his movements.

"Passengers for Rouen, take your seats!" a guard cried, and they got in. There was a slight whistle, followed by a loud whistle from the engine, which noisily puffed out its first jet of steam, while the wheels began to turn a little with a visible effort, and Rivet left the station and ran along by the track to get another look at Rosa, and as the carriage passed him, he began to crack his whip and to jump, while he sang at the top of his voice:

"How I regret
My dimpled arms,
My nimble legs,
And vanished charms."

And then he watched a white pocket-handkerchief, which somebody was waving, as it disappeared in the distance.

PART III

They slept the peaceful sleep of a quiet conscience, until they got to Rouen, and when they returned to the house, refreshed and rested, Madame Tellier could not help saying:

"It was all very well, but I was longing to get home."

They hurried over their supper, and then, when they had put on their usual evening costume, waited for their regular customers, and the little colored lamp outside the door told the passers-by that Madame Tellier had returned, and in a moment the news spread, nobody knew how or through whom.

Monsieur Philippe, the banker's son, even carried his friendliness so far as to send a special messenger to Monsieur Tournevau, who was in the bosom of his family.

The fish curer had several cousins to dinner every Sunday, and they were having coffee, when a man came in with a letter in his hand. Monsieur Tournevau was much excited; he opened the envelope and grew pale; it contained only these words in pencil:

"The cargo of cod has been found; the ship has come into port; good business for you. Come immediately."

He felt in his pockets, gave the messenger two sons, and suddenly blushing to his ears, he said: "I must go out." He handed his wife the laconic and mysterious note, rang the bell, and when the servant came in, he asked her to bring him has hat and overcoat immediately. As soon as he was in the street, he began to hurry, and the way seemed to him to be twice as long as usual, in consequence of his impatience.

Madame Tellier's establishment had put on quite a holiday look. On the ground floor, a number of sailors were making a deafening noise, and Louise and Flora drank with one and the other, and were being called for in every direction at once.

The upstairs room was full by nine o'clock. Monsieur Vasse, the Judge of the Tribunal of Commerce, Madame Tellier's regular but Platonic wooer, was talking to her in a corner in a low voice, and they were both smiling, as if they were about to come to an understanding.

Monsieur Poulin, the ex-mayor, was talking to Rosa, and she was running her hands through the old gentleman's white whiskers.

Tall Fernande was on the sofa, her feet on the coat of Monsieur Pinipesse, the tax collector, and leaning back against young Monsieur Philippe, her right arm around his neck, while she held a cigarette in her left hand.

Raphaele appeared to be talking seriously with Monsieur Dupuis, the insurance agent, and she finished by saying: "Yes, I will, yes."

Just then, the door opened suddenly, and Monsieur Tournevau came in, and was greeted with enthusiastic cries of "Long live Tournevau!" And Raphaele, who was dancing alone up and down the room, went and threw herself into his arms. He seized her in a vigorous embrace and, without saying a word, lifted her up as if she had been a feather.

Rosa was chatting to the ex-mayor, kissing him and puffing; both his whiskers at the same time, in order to keep his head straight.

Fernanad and Madame Tellier remained with the four men, and Monsieur Philippe exclaimed: "I will pay for some champagne; get three bottles, Madame Tellier." And Fernande gave him a hug, and whispered to him: "Play us a waltz, will you?" So he rose and sat down at the old piano in the corner, and managed to get a hoarse waltz out of the depths of the instrument.

The tall girl put her arms round the tax collector, Madame Tellier let Monsieur Vasse take her round the waist, and the two couples turned round, kissing as they danced. Monsieur Vasse, who had formerly danced in good society, waltzed with such elegance that Madame Tellier was quite captivated.

Frederic brought the champagne; the first cork popped, and Monsieur Philippe played the introduction to a quadrille, through which the four dancers walked in society fashion, decorously, with propriety, deportment, bows and curtsies, and then they began to drink.

Monsieur Philippe next struck up a lively polka, and Monsieur Tournevau started off with the handsome Jewess, whom he held without letting her feet touch the ground. Monsieur Pinipesse and Monsieur Vasse had started off with renewed vigor, and from time to time one or other couple would stop to toss off a long draught of sparkling wine, and that dance was threatening to become never-ending, when Rosa opened the door.

"I want to dance," she exclaimed. And she caught hold of Monsieur Dupuis, who was sitting idle on the couch, and the dance began again.

But the bottles were empty. "I will pay for one," Monsieur Tournevau said. "So will I," Monsieur Vasse declared. "And. I will do the same," Monsieur Dupuis remarked.

They all began to clap their hands, and it soon became a regular ball, and from time to time Louise and Flora ran upstairs quickly and had a few turns, while their customers downstairs grew impatient, and then they returned regretfully to the tap-room. At midnight they were still dancing.

Madame Tellier let them amuse themselves while she had long private talks in corners with Monsieur Vasse, as if to settle the last details of something that had already been settled.

At last, at one o'clock, the two married men, Monsieur Tournevau and Monsieur Pinipesse, declared that they were going home, and wanted to pay. Nothing was charged for except the champagne, and that cost only six francs a bottle, instead of ten, which was the usual price, and when they expressed their surprise at such generosity, Madame Tellier, who was beaming, said to them:

"We don't have a holiday every day."

DENIS

To Leon Chapron.

Marambot opened the letter which his servant Denis gave
him and smiled.

For twenty years Denis has been a servant in this house. He was
a short, stout, jovial man, who was known throughout the coun-
tryside as a model servant. He asked:

"Is monsieur pleased? Has monsieur received good news?"

M. Marambot was not rich. He was an old village druggist, a
bachelor, who lived on an income acquired with difficulty by sell-
ing drugs to the farmers. He answered:

"Yes, my boy. Old man Malois is afraid of the law-suit with
which I am threatening him. I shall get my money to-morrow.
Five thousand francs are not liable to harm the account of an old
bachelor."

M. Marambot rubbed his hands with satisfaction. He was a man
of quiet temperament, more sad than gay, incapable of any prolonged effort, careless in business.

He could undoubtedly have amassed a greater income had he
taken advantage of the deaths of colleagues established in more
important centers, by taking their places and carrying on their
business. But the trouble of moving and the thought of all the
preparations had always stopped him. After thinking the matter
over for a few days, he would be satisfied to say:

"Bah! I'll wait until the next time. I'll not lose anything by the
delay. I may even find something better."

Denis, on the contrary, was always urging his master to new
enterprises. Of an energetic temperament, he would continually
repeat:

"Oh! If I had only had the capital to start out with, I could have
made a fortune! One thousand francs would do me."

M. Marambot would smile without answering and would go
out in his little garden, where, his hands behind his back, he
would walk about dreaming.

All day long, Denis sang the joyful refrains of the folk-songs of
the district. He even showed an unusual activity, for he cleaned
all the windows of the house, energetically rubbing the glass, and

singing at the top of his voice.

M. Marambot, surprised at his zeal, said to him several times, smiling:

"My boy, if you work like that there will be nothing left for you to do to-morrow."

The following day, at about nine o'clock in the morning, the postman gave Denis four letters for his master, one of them very heavy. M. Marambot immediately shut himself up in his room until late in the afternoon. He then handed his servant four letters for the mail. One of them was addressed to M. Malois; it was undoubtedly a receipt for the money.

Denis asked his master no questions; he appeared to be as sad and gloomy that day as he had seemed joyful the day before.

Night came. M. Marambot went to bed as usual and slept.

He was awakened by a strange noise. He sat up in his bed and listened. Suddenly the door opened, and Denis appeared, holding in one hand a candle and in the other a carving knife, his eyes staring, his face contracted as though moved by some deep emotion; he was as pale as a ghost.

M. Marambot, astonished, thought that he was sleep-walking, and he was going to get out of bed and assist him when the servant blew out the light and rushed for the bed. His master stretched out his hands to receive the shock which knocked him over on his back; he was trying to seize the hands of his servant, whom he now thought to be crazy, in order to avoid the blows which the latter was aiming at him.

He was struck by the knife; once in the shoulder, once in the forehead and the third time in the chest. He fought wildly, waving his arms around in the darkness, kicking and crying:

"Denis! Denis! Are you mad? Listen, Denis!"

But the latter, gasping for breath, kept up his furious attack always striking, always repulsed, sometimes with a kick, sometimes with a punch, and rushing forward again furiously.

M. Marambot was wounded twice more, once in the leg and once in the stomach. But, suddenly, a thought flashed across his mind, and he began to shriek:

"Stop, stop, Denis, I have not yet received my money!"

The man immediately ceased, and his master could hear his labored breathing in the darkness.

M. Marambot then went on:

"I have received nothing. M. Malois takes back what he said, the law-suit will take place; that is why you carried the letters to the mail. Just read those on my desk."

With a final effort, he reached for his matches and lit the candle.

He was covered with blood. His sheets, his curtains, and even the walls, were spattered with red. Denis, standing in the middle of the room, was also bloody from head to foot.

When he saw the blood, M. Marambot thought himself dead, and fell unconscious.

At break of day he revived. It was some time, however, before he regained his senses, and was able to understand or remember. But, suddenly, the memory of the attack and of his wounds returned to him, and he was filled with such terror that he closed his eyes in order not to see anything. After a few minutes he grew calmer and began to think. He had not died immediately, therefore he might still recover. He felt weak, very weak; but he had no real pain, although he noticed an uncomfortable smarting sensation in several parts of his body. He also felt icy cold, and all wet, and as though wrapped up in bandages. He thought that this dampness came from the blood which he had lost; and he shivered at the dreadful thought of this red liquid which had come from his veins and covered his bed. The idea of seeing this terrible spectacle again so upset him that he kept his eyes closed with all his strength, as though they might open in spite of himself.

What had become of Denis? He had probably escaped.

But what could he, Marambot, do now? Get up? Call for help? But if he should make the slightest motions, his wounds would undoubtedly open up again and he would die from loss of blood.

Suddenly he heard the door of his room open. His heart almost stopped. It was certainly Denis who was coming to finish him up. He held his breath in order to make the murderer think that he had been successful.

He felt his sheet being lifted up, and then someone feeling his stomach. A sharp pain near his hip made him start. He was being very gently washed with cold water. Therefore, someone must have discovered the misdeed and he was being cared for. A wild joy seized him; but prudently, he did not wish to show that he was conscious. He opened one eye, just one, with the greatest precaution.

He recognized Denis standing beside him, Denis himself! Mercy! He hastily closed his eye again.

Denis! What could he be doing? What did he want? What awful scheme could he now be carrying out?

What was he doing? Well, he was washing him in order to hide the traces of his crime! And he would now bury him in the garden, under ten feet of earth, so that no one could discover him!

Or perhaps under the wine cellar! And M. Marambot began to tremble like a leaf. He kept saying to himself: "I am lost, lost!" He closed his eyes so as not to see the knife as it descended for the final stroke. It did not come. Denis was now lifting him up and bandaging him. Then he began carefully to dress the wound on his leg, as his master had taught him to do.

There was no longer any doubt. His servant, after wishing to kill him, was trying to save him.

Then M. Marambot, in a dying voice, gave him the practical piece of advice:

"Wash the wounds in a dilute solution of carbolic acid!"

Denis answered:

"This is what I am doing, monsieur."

M. Marambot opened both his eyes. There was no sign of blood either on the bed, on the walls, or on the murderer. The wounded man was stretched out on clean white sheets.

The two men looked at each other.

Finally M. Marambot said calmly:

"You have been guilty of a great crime."

Denis answered:

"I am trying to make up for it, monsieur. If you will not tell on me, I will serve you as faithfully as in the past."

This was no time to anger his servant. M. Marambot murmured as he closed his eyes:

"I swear not to tell on you."

Denis saved his master. He spent days and nights without sleep, never leaving the sick room, preparing drugs, broths, potions, feeling his pulse, anxiously counting the beats, attending him with the skill of a trained nurse and the devotion of a son.

He continually asked:

"Well, monsieur, how do you feel?"

M. Marambot would answer in a weak voice:

"A little better, my boy, thank you."

And when the sick man would wake up at night, he would often see his servant seated in an armchair, weeping silently.

Never had the old druggist been so cared for, so fondled, so spoiled. At first he had said to himself:

"As soon as I am well I shall get rid of this rascal."

He was now convalescing, and from day to day he would put off dismissing his murderer. He thought that no one would ever show him such care and attention, for he held this man through fear; and he warned him that he had left a document with a lawyer denouncing him to the law if any new accident should occur.

This precaution seemed to guarantee him against any future attack; and he then asked himself if it would not be wiser to keep this man near him, in order to watch him closely.

Just as formerly, when he would hesitate about taking some larger place of business, he could not make up his mind to any decision.

"There is always time," he would say to himself.

Denis continued to show himself an admirable servant. M. Marambot was well. He kept him.

One morning, just as he was finishing breakfast, he suddenly heard a great noise in the kitchen. He hastened in there. Denis was struggling with two gendarmes. An officer was taking notes on his pad.

As soon as he saw his master, the servant began to sob, exclaiming:

"You told on me, monsieur, that's not right, after what you had promised me. You have broken your word of honor, Monsieur Marambot; that is not right, that's not right!"

M. Marambot, bewildered and distressed at being suspected, lifted his hand:

"I swear to you before the Lord, my boy that I did not tell on you. I haven't the slightest idea how the police could have found out about your attack on me."

The officer started:

"You say that he attacked you, M. Marambot?"

The bewildered druggist answered:

"Yes—but I did not tell on him—I haven't said a word—I swear it—he has served me excellently from that time on—"

The officer pronounced severely:

"I will take down your testimony. The law will take notice of this new action, of which it was ignorant, Monsieur Marambot. I was commissioned to arrest your servant for the theft of two ducks surreptitiously taken by him from M. Duhamel of which act there are witnesses. I shall make a note of your information."

Then, turning toward his men, he ordered:

"Come on, bring him along!"

The two gendarmes dragged Denis out.

The lawyer used a plea of insanity, contrasting the two misdeeds in order to strengthen his argument. He had clearly proved that the theft of the two ducks came from the same mental condition as the eight knife-wounds in the body of Maramlot. He had cunningly analyzed all the phases of this transitory condition of mental aberration, which could, doubtless, be cured by a few months' treatment in a reputable sanatorium. He had spoken in enthusiastic terms of the continued devotion of this faithful servant, of the care with which he had surrounded his master, wounded by him in a moment of alienation.

Touched by this memory, M. Marambot felt the tears rising to his eyes.

The lawyer noticed it, opened his arms with a broad gesture, spreading out the long black sleeves of his robe like the wings of a bat, and exclaimed:

"Look, look, gentleman of the jury, look at those tears. What more can I say for my client? What speech, what argument, what reasoning would be worth these tears of his master? They, speak louder than I do, louder than the law; they cry: 'Mercy, for the poor wandering mind of a while ago! They implore, they pardon, they bless!"

He was silent and sat down.

Then the judge, turning to Marambot, whose testimony had been excellent for his servant, asked him:

"But, monsieur, even admitting that you consider this man insane, that does not explain why you should have kept him. He was none the less dangerous."

Marambot, wiping his eyes, answered:

"Well, your honor, what can you expect? Nowadays it's so hard to find good servants—I could never have found a better one."

Denis was acquitted and put in a sanatorium at his master's expense.

MY WIFE

*J*t had been a stag dinner. These men still came together once in a while without their wives as they had done when they were bachelors. They would eat for a long time, drink for a long time; they would talk of everything, stir up those old and joyful memories which bring a smile to the lip and a tremor to the heart. One of them was saying: "Georges, do you remember our excursion to Saint-Germain with those two little girls from Montmartre?"

"I should say I do!"

And a little detail here or there would be remembered, and all these things brought joy to the hearts.

The conversation turned on marriage, and each one said with a sincere air: "Oh, if it were to do over again!" Georges Duportin added: "It's strange how easily one falls into it. You have fully decided never to marry; and then, in the springtime, you go to the country; the weather is warm; the summer is beautiful; the fields are full of flowers; you meet a young girl at some friend's house—crash! all is over. You return married!"

Pierre Letoile exclaimed: "Correct! that is exactly my case, only there were some peculiar incidents—"

His friend interrupted him: "As for you, you have no cause to complain. You have the most charming wife in the world, pretty, amiable, perfect! You are undoubtedly the happiest one of us all."

The other one continued: "It's not my fault."

"How so?"

"It is true that I have a perfect wife, but I certainly married her much against my will."

"Nonsense!"

"Yes—this is the adventure. I was thirty-five, and I had no more idea of marrying than I had of hanging myself. Young girls seemed to me to be inane, and I loved pleasure.

"During the month of May I was invited to the wedding of my cousin, Simon d'Erabel, in Normandy. It was a regular Normandy wedding. We sat down at the table at five o'clock in the evening and at eleven o'clock we were still eating. I had been paired off, for the occasion, with a Mademoiselle Dumoulin, daughter of a retired colonel, a young, blond, soldierly person, well formed, frank and talkative. She took complete possession of me for the whole day, dragged me into the park, made me dance willy-nilly, bored me to death. I said to myself: 'That's all very well for to-day, but tomorrow I'll get out. That's all there is to it!'

"Toward eleven o'clock at night the women retired to their rooms; the men stayed, smoking while they drank or drinking while they smoked, whichever you will.

"Through the open window we could see the country folks dancing. Farmers and peasant girls were jumping about in a circle yelling at the top of their lungs a dance air which was feebly accompanied by two violins and a clarinet. The wild song of the peasants often completely drowned the sound of the instruments, and the weak music, interrupted by the unrestrained voices, seemed to come to us in little fragments of scattered notes. Two enormous casks, surrounded by flaming torches, contained drinks for the crowd. Two men were kept busy rinsing the glasses or bowls in a bucket and immediately holding them under the spigots, from which flowed the red stream of wine or the golden stream of pure cider; and the parched dancers, the old ones quietly, the girls panting, came up, stretched out their arms and grasped some receptacle, threw back their heads and poured down their throats the drink which they preferred. On a table were bread, butter, cheese and sausages. Each one would step up from time to time and swallow a mouthful, and under the starlit sky this healthy and violent exercise was a pleasing sight, and made one also feel like drinking from these enormous casks and eating the crisp bread and butter with a raw onion.

"A mad desire seized me to take part in this merrymaking, and I left my companions. I must admit that I was probably a little tipsy, but I was soon entirely so.

"I grabbed the hand of a big, panting peasant woman and I jumped her about until I was out of breath.

"Then I drank some wine and reached for another girl. In order to refresh myself afterward, I swallowed a bowlful of cider, and I began to bounce around as if possessed.

"I was very light on my feet. The boys, delighted, were watching me and trying to imitate me; the girls all wished to dance with me, and jumped about heavily with the grace of cows.

"After each dance I drank a glass of wine or a glass of cider, and toward two o'clock in the morning I was so drunk that I could hardly stand up.

"I realized my condition and tried to reach my room. Everybody was asleep and the house was silent and dark.

"I had no matches and everybody was in bed. As soon as I reached the vestibule I began to, feel dizzy. I had a lot of trouble to find the banister. At last, by accident, my hand came in contact with it, and I sat down on the first step of the stairs in order to try to gather my scattered wits.

"My room was on the second floor; it was the third door to the left. Fortunately I had not forgotten that. Armed with this knowledge, I arose, not without difficulty, and I began to ascend, step by step. In my hands I firmly gripped the iron railing in order not to fall, and took great pains to make no noise.

"Only three or four times did my foot miss the steps, and I went down on my knees; but thanks to the energy of my arms and the strength of my will, I avoided falling completely.

"At last I reached the second floor and I set out in my journey along the hall, feeling my way by the walls. I felt one door; I counted: 'One'; but a sudden dizziness made me lose my hold on the wall, make a strange turn and fall up against the other wall. I wished to turn in a straight line: The crossing was long and full of hardships. At last I reached the shore, and, prudently, I began to travel along again until I met another door. In order to be sure to make no mistake, I again counted out loud: 'Two.' I started out on my walk again. At last I found the third door. I said: 'Three, that's my room,' and I turned the knob. The door opened. Notwithstanding my befuddled state, I thought: 'Since the door opens, this must be home.' After softly closing the door, I stepped out in the darkness. I bumped against something soft: my easy-chair. I immediately stretched myself out on it.

"In my condition it would not have been wise to look for my bureau, my candles, my matches. It would have taken me at least two hours. It would probably have taken me that long also to undress; and even then I might not have succeeded. I gave it up.

"I only took my shoes off; I unbuttoned my waistcoat, which was choking me, I loosened my trousers and went to sleep.

"This undoubtedly lasted for a long time. I was suddenly awakened by a deep voice which was saying: 'What, you lazy girl, still in bed? It's ten o'clock!'

"A woman's voice answered: 'Already! I was so tired yesterday.'

"In bewilderment I wondered what this dialogue meant. Where was I? What had I done? My mind was wandering, still surrounded by a heavy fog. The first voice continued: 'I'm going to raise your curtains.'

"I heard steps approaching me. Completely at a loss what to do, I sat up. Then a hand was placed on my head. I started. The voice asked: 'Who is there?' I took good care not to answer. A furious grasp seized me. I in turn seized him, and a terrific struggle ensued. We were rolling around, knocking over the furniture and crashing against the walls. A woman's voice was shrieking: 'Help! help!'

"Servants, neighbors, frightened women crowded around us. The blinds were open and the shades drawn. I was struggling with Colonel Dumoulin.

"I had slept beside his daughter's bed!

"When we were separated, I escaped to my room, dumbfounded. I locked myself in and sat down with my feet on a chair, for my shoes had been left in the young girl's room.

"I heard a great noise through the whole house, doors being opened and closed, whisperings and rapid steps.

"After half an hour some one knocked on my door. I cried: 'Who is there?' It was my uncle, the bridegroom's father. I opened the door:

"He was pale and furious, and he treated me harshly: 'You have behaved like a scoundrel in my house, do you hear?' Then he added more gently 'But, you young fool, why the devil did you let yourself get caught at ten o'clock in the morning? You go to sleep like a log in that room, instead of leaving immediately—immediately after.'

"I exclaimed: 'But, uncle, I assure you that nothing occurred. I was drunk and got into the wrong room.'

"He shrugged his shoulders! 'Don't talk nonsense.' I raised my hand, exclaiming: 'I swear to you on my honor.' My uncle continued: 'Yes, that's all right. It's your duty to say that.'

"I in turn grew angry and told him the whole unfortunate occurrence. He looked at me with a bewildered expression, not knowing what to believe. Then he went out to confer with the colonel.

"I heard that a kind of jury of the mothers had been formed, to which were submitted the different phases of the situation.

"He came back an hour later, sat down with the dignity of a judge and began: 'No matter what may be the situation, I can see only one way out of it for you; it is to marry Mademoiselle Dumoulin.'

"I bounded out of the chair, crying: 'Never! never!'

"Gravely he asked: 'Well, what do you expect to do?'

"I answered simply: 'Why—leave as soon as my shoes are returned to me.'

"My uncle continued: 'Please do not jest. The colonel has decided to blow your brains out as soon as he sees you. And you may be sure that he does not threaten idly. I spoke of a duel and he answered: "No, I tell you that I will blow his brains out."'

"'Let us now examine the question from another point of view. Either you have misbehaved yourself—and then so much the worse for you, my boy; one should not go near a young girl—or else, being drunk, as you say, you made a mistake in the room. In this case, it's even worse for you. You shouldn't get yourself into such foolish situations. Whatever you may say, the poor girl's reputation is lost, for a drunkard's excuses are never believed. The only real victim in the matter is the girl. Think it over.'

"He went away, while I cried after him: 'Say what you will, I'll not marry her!'

"I stayed alone for another hour. Then my aunt came. She was crying. She used every argument. No one believed my story. They could not imagine that this young girl could have forgotten to lock her door in a house full of company. The colonel had struck her. She had been crying the whole morning. It was a terrible and unforgettable scandal. And my good aunt added: 'Ask for her hand, anyhow. We may, perhaps, find some way out of it when we are drawing up the papers.'

"This prospect relieved me. And I agreed to write my proposal. An hour later I left for Paris. The following day I was informed that I had been accepted.

"Then, in three weeks, before I had been able to find any excuse, the banns were published, the announcement sent out, the contract signed, and one Monday morning I found myself in a church, beside a weeping young girl, after telling the magistrate that I consented to take her as my companion—for better, for worse.

"I had not seen her since my adventure, and I glanced at her out of the corner of my eye with a certain malevolent surprise. However, she was not ugly—far from it. I said to myself: 'There is some one who won't laugh every day.'

"She did not look at me once until, the evening, and she did not say a single word.

"Toward the middle of the night I entered the bridal chamber with the full intention of letting her know my resolutions, for I was now master. I found her sitting in an armchair, fully dressed, pale and with red eyes. As soon as I entered she rose and came slowly toward me saying: 'Monsieur, I am ready to do whatever you may command. I will kill myself if you so desire'

"The colonel's daughter was as pretty as she could be in this heroic role. I kissed her; it was my privilege.

"I soon saw that I had not got a bad bargain. I have now been married five years. I do not regret it in the least."

Pierre Letoile was silent. His companions were laughing. One of them said: "Marriage is indeed a lottery; you must never choose your numbers. The haphazard ones are the best."

Another added by way of conclusion: "Yes, but do not forget that the god of drunkards chose for Pierre."

THE UNKNOWN

We were speaking of adventures, and each one of us was relating his story of delightful experiences, surprising meetings, on the train, in a hotel, at the seashore. According to Roger des Annettes, the seashore was particularly favorable to the little blind god.

Gontran, who was keeping mum, was asked what he thought of it.

"I guess Paris is about the best place for that," he said. "Woman is like a precious trinket, we appreciate her all the more when we meet her in the most unexpected places; but the rarest ones are only to be found in Paris."

He was silent for a moment, and then continued:

"By Jove, it's great! Walk along the streets on some spring morning. The little women, daintily tripping along, seem to blossom out like flowers. What a delightful, charming sight! The dainty perfume of violet is everywhere. The city is gay, and everybody notices the women. By Jove, how tempting they are in their light, thin dresses, which occasionally give one a glimpse of the delicate pink flesh beneath!

"One saunters along, head up, mind alert, and eyes open. I tell you it's great! You see her in the distance, while still a block away; you already know that she is going to please you at closer quarters. You can recognize her by the flower on her hat, the toss of her head, or her gait. She approaches, and you say to yourself: 'Look out, here she is!' You come closer to her and you devour her with your eyes.

"Is it a young girl running errands for some store, a young woman returning from church, or hastening to see her lover? What do you care? Her well-rounded bosom shows through the thin waist. Oh, if you could only take her in your arms and fondle and kiss her! Her glance may be timid or bold, her hair light or dark. What difference does it make? She brushes against you, and a cold shiver runs down your spine. Ah, how you wish for her all day! How many of these dear creatures have I met this way, and how wildly in love I would have been had I known them more intimately.

"Have you ever noticed that the ones we would love the most distractedly are those whom we never meet to know? Curious, isn't it? From time to time we barely catch a glimpse of some woman, the mere sight of whom thrills our senses. But it goes no further. When I think of all the adorable creatures that I have elbowed in the streets of Paris, I fairly rave. Who are they! Where are they? Where can I find them again? There is a proverb which says that happiness often passes our way; I am sure that I have often passed alongside the one who could have caught me like a linnet in the snare of her fresh beauty."

Roger des Annettes had listened smilingly. He answered: "I know that as well as you do. This is what happened to me: About five years ago, for the first time I met, on the Pont de la Concorde, a young woman who made a wonderful impression on me. She was dark, rather stout, with glossy hair, and eyebrows which nearly met above two dark eyes. On her lip was a scarcely perceptible down, which made one dream-dream as one dreams of beloved woods, on seeing a bunch of wild violets. She had a small waist and a well-developed bust, which seemed to present a challenge, offer a temptation. Her eyes were like two black spots on white enamel. Her glance was strange, vacant, unthinking, and yet wonderfully beautiful.

"I imagined that she might be a Jewess. I followed her, and then turned round to look at her, as did many others. She walked with a swinging gait that was not graceful, but somehow attracted one. At the Place de la Concorde she took a carriage, and I stood there like a fool, moved by the strongest desire that had ever assailed me.

"For about three weeks I thought only of her; and then her memory passed out of my mind.

"Six months later I descried her in the Rue de la Paix again. On seeing her I felt the same shock that one experiences on seeing a once dearly loved woman. I stopped that I might better observe her. When she passed close enough to touch me I felt as though I were standing before a red hot furnace. Then, when she had passed by, I noticed a delicious sensation, as of a cooling breeze blowing over my face. I did not follow her. I was afraid of doing something foolish. I was afraid of myself.

"She haunted all my dreams.

"It was a year before I saw her again. But just as the sun was going down on one beautiful evening in May I recognized her walking along the Avenue des Champs-Elysees. The Arc de Triomphe stood out in bold relief against the fiery glow of the sky.

A golden haze filled the air; it was one of those delightful spring evenings which are the glory of Paris.

"I followed her, tormented by a desire to address her, to kneel before her, to pour forth the emotion which was choking me. Twice I passed by her only to fall back, and each time as I passed by I felt this sensation, as of scorching heat, which I had noticed in the Rue de la Paix.

"She glanced at me, and then I saw her enter a house on the Rue de Presbourg. I waited for her two hours and she did not come out. Then I decided to question the janitor. He seemed not to understand me. 'She must be visiting some one,' he said.

"The next time I was eight months without seeing her. But one freezing morning in January, I was walking along the Boulevard Malesherbes at a dog trot, so as to keep warm, when at the corner I bumped into a woman and knocked a small package out of her hand. I tried to apologize. It was she!

"At first I stood stock still from the shock; then having returned to her the package which she had dropped, I said abruptly:

"'I am both grieved and delighted, madame, to have jostled you. For more than two years I have known you, admired you, and had the most ardent wish to be presented to you; nevertheless I have been unable to find out who you are, or where you live. Please excuse these foolish words. Attribute them to a passionate desire to be numbered among your acquaintances. Such sentiments can surely offend you in no way! You do not know me. My name is Baron Roger des Annettes. Make inquiries about me, and you will find that I am a gentleman. Now, if you refuse my request, you will throw me into abject misery. Please be good to me and tell me how I can see you.'

"She looked at me with her strange vacant stare, and answered smilingly:

"'Give me your address. I will come and see you.'

"I was so dumfounded that I must have shown my surprise. But I quickly gathered my wits together and gave her a visiting card, which she slipped into her pocket with a quick, deft movement.

"Becoming bolder, I stammered:

"'When shall I see you again?'

"She hesitated, as though mentally running over her list of engagements, and then murmured:

"'Will Sunday morning suit you?'

"'I should say it would!'

"She went on, after having stared at me, judged, weighed and analyzed me with this heavy and vacant gaze which seemed to leave a quieting and deadening impression on the person towards whom it was directed.

"Until Sunday my mind was occupied day and night trying to guess who she might be and planning my course of conduct towards her. I finally decided to buy her a jewel, a beautiful little jewel, which I placed in its box on the mantelpiece, and left it there awaiting her arrival.

"I spent a restless night waiting for her.

"At ten o'clock she came, calm and quiet, and with her hand outstretched, as though she had known me for years. Drawing up a chair, I took her hat and coat and furs, and laid them aside. And then, timidly, I took her hand in mine; after that all went on without a hitch.

"Ah, my friends! what a bliss it is, to stand at a discreet distance and watch the hidden pink and blue ribbons, partly concealed, to observe the hazy lines of the beloved one's form, as they become visible through the last of the filmy garments! What a delight it is to watch the ostrich-like modesty of those who are in reality none too modest. And what is so pretty as their motions!

"Her back was turned towards me, and suddenly, my eyes were irresistibly drawn to a large black spot right between her shoulders. What could it be? Were my eyes deceiving me? But no, there it was, staring me in the face! Then my mind reverted to the faint down on her lip, the heavy eyebrows almost meeting over her coal-black eyes, her glossy black hair —I should have been prepared for some surprise.

"Nevertheless I was dumfounded, and my mind was haunted by dim visions of strange adventures. I seemed to see before me one of the evil genii of the Thousand and One Nights, one of these dangerous and crafty creatures whose mission it is to drag men down to unknown depths. I thought of Solomon, who made the Queen of Sheba walk on a mirror that he might be sure that her feet were not cloven.

"And when the time came for me to sing of love to her, my voice forsook me. At first she showed surprise, which soon turned to anger; and she said, quickly putting on her wraps:

"'It was hardly worth while for me to go out of my way to come here.'

"I wanted her to accept the ring which I had bought for her, but she replied haughtily: 'For whom do you take me, sir?' I blushed to the roots of my hair. She left without saying another word.

"There is my whole adventure. But the worst part of it is that I am now madly in love with her. I can't see a woman without thinking of her. All the others disgust me, unless they remind me of her. I cannot kiss a woman without seeing her face before me, and without suffering the torture of unsatisfied desire. She is always with me, always there, dressed or nude, my true love. She is there, beside the other one, visible but intangible. I am almost willing to believe that she was bewitched, and carried a talisman between her shoulders.

"Who is she? I don't know yet. I have met her once or twice since. I bowed, but she pretended not to recognize me. Who is she? An Oriental? Yes, doubtless an oriental Jewess! I believe that she must be a Jewess! But why? Why? I don't know!"

THE APPARITION

The subject of sequestration of the person came up in speaking of a recent lawsuit, and each of us had a story to tell—a true story, he said. We had been spending the evening together at an old family mansion in the Rue de Grenelle, just a party of intimate friends. The old Marquis de la Tour-Samuel, who was eighty-two, rose, and, leaning his elbow on the mantelpiece, said in his somewhat shaky voice:

"I also know of something strange, so strange that it has haunted me all my life. It is now fifty-six years since the incident occurred, and yet not a month passes that I do not see it again in a dream, so great is the impression of fear it has left on my mind. For ten minutes I experienced such horrible fright that ever since then a sort of constant terror has remained with me. Sudden noises startle me violently, and objects imperfectly distinguished at night inspire me with a mad desire to flee from them. In short, I am afraid of the dark!

"But I would not have acknowledged that before I reached my present age. Now I can say anything. I have never receded before real danger, ladies. It is, therefore, permissible, at eighty-two years of age, not to be brave in presence of imaginary danger.

"That affair so completely upset me, caused me such deep and mysterious and terrible distress, that I never spoke of it to any one. I will now tell it to you exactly as it happened, without any attempt at explanation.

"In July, 1827, I was stationed at Rouen. One day as I was walking along the quay I met a man whom I thought I recognized without being able to recall exactly who he was. Instinctively I made a movement to stop. The stranger perceived it and at once extended his hand.

"He was a friend to whom I had been deeply attached as a youth. For five years I had not seen him; he seemed to have aged half a century. His hair was quite white and he walked bent over as though completely exhausted. He apparently understood my surprise, and he told me of the misfortune which had shattered his life.

"Having fallen madly in love with a young girl, he had married her, but after a year of more than earthly happiness she died suddenly of an affection of the heart. He left his country home on the very day of her burial and came to his town house in Rouen, where he lived, alone and unhappy, so sad and wretched that he thought constantly of suicide.

"'Since I have found you again in this manner,' he said, 'I will ask you to render me an important service. It is to go and get me out of the desk in my bedroom—our bedroom—some papers of which I have urgent need. I cannot send a servant or a business clerk, as discretion and absolute silence are necessary. As for myself, nothing on earth would induce me to reenter that house. I will give you the key of the room, which I myself locked on leaving, and the key of my desk, also a few words for my gardener, telling him to open the chateau for you. But come and breakfast with me tomorrow and we will arrange all that.'

"I promised to do him the slight favor he asked. It was, for that matter, only a ride which I could make in an hour on horseback, his property being but a few miles distant from Rouen.

"At ten o'clock the following day I breakfasted, tete-a-tete, with my friend, but he scarcely spoke.

"He begged me to pardon him; the thought of the visit I was about to make to that room, the scene of his dead happiness, overcame him, he said. He, indeed, seemed singularly agitated and preoccupied, as though undergoing some mysterious mental struggle.

"At length he explained to me exactly what I had to do. It was very simple. I must take two packages of letters and a roll of papers from the first right-hand drawer of the desk, of which I had the key. He added:

"'I need not beg you to refrain from glancing at them.'

"I was wounded at that remark and told him so somewhat sharply. He stammered:

"'Forgive me, I suffer so,' and tears came to his eyes.

"At about one o'clock I took leave of him to accomplish my mission.

"'The weather was glorious, and I trotted across the fields, listening to the song of the larks and the rhythmical clang of my sword against my boot. Then I entered the forest and walked my horse. Branches of trees caressed my face as I passed, and now and then I caught a leaf with my teeth and chewed it, from sheer gladness of heart at being alive and vigorous on such a radiant day.

"As I approached the chateau I took from my pocket the letter I had for the gardener, and was astonished at finding it sealed. I was so irritated that I was about to turn back without having fulfilled my promise, but reflected that I should thereby display undue susceptibility. My friend in his troubled condition might easily have fastened the envelope without noticing that he did so.

"The manor looked as if it had been abandoned for twenty years. The open gate was falling from its hinges, the walks were overgrown with grass and the flower beds were no longer distinguishable.

"The noise I made by kicking at a shutter brought out an old man from a side door. He seemed stunned with astonishment at seeing me. On receiving my letter, he read it, reread it, turned it over and over, looked me up and down, put the paper in his pocket and finally said:

"'Well, what is it you wish?'

"I replied shortly:

"'You ought to know, since you have just read your master's orders. I wish to enter the chateau.'

"He seemed overcome.

"'Then you are going in—into her room?'

"I began to lose patience.

"'Damn it! Are you presuming to question me?'

"He stammered in confusion:

"'No—sir—but—but it has not been opened since—since the death. If you will be kind enough to wait five minutes I will go and—and see if—'

"I interrupted him angrily:

"'See here, what do you mean by your tricks?

"'You know very well you cannot enter the room, since here is the key!'

"He no longer objected.

"'Then, sir, I will show you the way.'

"'Show me the staircase and leave me. I'll find my way without you.'

"'But—sir—indeed—'

"This time I lost patience, and pushing him aside, went into the house.

"I first went through the kitchen, then two rooms occupied by this man and his wife. I then crossed a large hall, mounted a staircase and recognized the door described by my friend.

"I easily opened it, and entered the apartment. It was so dark that at first I could distinguish nothing. I stopped short, disagreeably affected by that disagreeable, musty odor of closed, unoccupied rooms. As my eyes slowly became accustomed to the darkness I saw plainly enough a large and disordered bedroom, the bed without sheets but still retaining its mattresses and pillows, on one of which was a deep impression, as though an elbow or a head had recently rested there.

"The chairs all seemed out of place. I noticed that a door, doubtless that of a closet, had remained half open.

"I first went to the window, which I opened to let in the light, but the fastenings of the shutters had grown so rusty that I could not move them. I even tried to break them with my sword, but without success. As I was growing irritated over my useless efforts and could now see fairly well in the semi-darkness, I gave up the hope of getting more light, and went over to the writing desk.

"I seated myself in an armchair and, letting down the lid of the desk, I opened the drawer designated. It was full to the top. I needed but three packages, which I knew how to recognize, and began searching for them.

"I was straining my eyes in the effort to read the superscriptions when I seemed to hear, or, rather, feel, something rustle back of me. I paid no attention, believing that a draught from the window was moving some drapery. But in a minute or so another movement, almost imperceptible, sent a strangely disagreeable little shiver over my skin. It was so stupid to be affected, even slightly, that self-respect prevented my turning around. I had just found the second package I needed and was about to lay my hand on the third when a long and painful sigh, uttered just at my shoulder, made me bound like a madman from my seat and land several feet off. As I jumped I had turned round my hand on the hilt of my sword, and, truly, if I had not felt it at my side I should have taken to my heels like a coward.

"A tall woman dressed in white, stood gazing at me from the back of the chair where I had been sitting an instant before.

"Such a shudder ran through all my limbs that I nearly fell backward. No one who has not experienced it can understand that frightful, unreasoning terror! The mind becomes vague, the heart ceases to beat, the entire body grows as limp as a sponge.

"I do not believe in ghosts, nevertheless I collapsed from a hideous dread of the dead, and I suffered, oh! I suffered in a few moments more than in all the rest of my life from the irresistible terror of the supernatural. If she had not spoken I should have died perhaps. But she spoke, she spoke in a sweet, sad voice that set my nerves vibrating. I dare not say that I became master of myself and recovered my reason. No! I was terrified and scarcely knew what I was doing. But a certain innate pride, a remnant of soldierly instinct, made me, almost in spite of myself, maintain a bold front. She said:

"'Oh, sir, you can render me a great service.'

"I wanted to reply, but it was impossible for me to pronounce a word. Only a vague sound came from my throat. She continued:

"'Will you? You can save me, cure me. I suffer frightfully. I suffer, oh! how I suffer!' and she slowly seated herself in my armchair, still looking at me.

"'Will you?' she said.

"I nodded in assent, my voice still being paralyzed.

"Then she held out to me a tortoise-shell comb and murmured:

"'Comb my hair, oh! comb my hair; that will cure me; it must be combed. Look at my head—how I suffer; and my hair pulls so!'

"Her hair, unbound, very long and very black, it seemed to me, hung over the back of the armchair and touched the floor.

"Why did I promise? Why did I take that comb with a shudder, and why did I hold in my hands her long black hair that gave my skin a frightful cold sensation, as though I were handling snakes? I cannot tell.

"That sensation has remained in my fingers, and I still tremble in recalling it.

"I combed her hair. I handled, I know not how, those icy locks. I twisted, knotted, and unknotted, and braided them. She sighed, bowed her head, seemed happy. Suddenly she said, 'Thank you!' snatched the comb from my hands and fled by the door that I had noticed ajar.

"Left alone, I experienced for several seconds the horrible agitation of one who awakens from a nightmare. At length I regained my senses. I ran to the window and with a mighty effort burst open the shutters, letting a flood of light into the room. Immediately I sprang to the door by which that being had departed. I found it closed and immovable!

"Then the mad desire to flee overcame me like a panic the panic which soldiers know in battle. I seized the three packets of letters on the open desk, ran from the room, dashed down the stairs four steps at a time, found myself outside, I know not how, and, perceiving my horse a few steps off, leaped into the saddle and galloped away.

"I stopped only when I reached Rouen and alighted at my lodgings. Throwing the reins to my orderly, I fled to my room and shut myself in to reflect. For an hour I anxiously asked myself if I were not the victim of a hallucination. Undoubtedly I had had one of those incomprehensible nervous attacks those exaltations of mind that give rise to visions and are the stronghold of the supernatural. And I was about to believe I had seen a vision, had a hallucination, when, as I approached the window, my eyes fell, by chance, upon my breast. My military cape was covered with long black hairs! One by one, with trembling fingers, I plucked them off and threw them away.

"I then called my orderly. I was too disturbed, too upset to go and see my friend that day, and I also wished to reflect more fully upon what I ought to tell him. I sent him his letters, for which he gave the soldier a receipt. He asked after me most particularly, and, on being told I was ill—had had a sunstroke—appeared exceedingly anxious. Next morning I went to him, determined to tell him the truth. He had gone out the evening before and had not yet returned. I called again during the day; my friend was still absent. After waiting a week longer without news of him, I notified the authorities and a judicial search was instituted. Not the slightest trace of his whereabouts or manner of disappearance was discovered.

"A minute inspection of the abandoned chateau revealed nothing of a suspicious character. There was no indication that a woman had been concealed there.

"After fruitless researches all further efforts were abandoned, and for fifty-six years I have heard nothing; I know no more than before."

CPSIA information can be obtained
at www.ICGtesting.com
Printed in the USA
LVHW041821140720
660698LV00025B/679

9 781641 817455